TERENCE S

DUNGEON L ____
The Correct Sadist II

velvet

DUNGEON EVIDENCE
The Correct Sadist II
Terence Sellers
Published 1997
by
Velvet Publications
83 Clerkenwell Road
London EC1, UK
ISBN 1 871592 58 5
Copyright © Terence Sellers 1997
Cover photograph:
Copyright © Richelle Simpson-Little 1997
Design:
Bradley Davis/Sailorboy PCP
A Bondagebest Production

CONTENTS

PART ONE
THE LOGIC OF THE ARCANUM
7

PART TWO
THE CASE STUDIES OF DR. ANGEL STERN
31

PART THREE
OUR POOR PROGNOSIS
159

THE LOGIC
OF THE ARCANUM

(or)
The Arguments Of Sadomasochism

the theatrical dungeon

Let us sink into darkness with our eyes sealed shut; let us enter that room where no-one ever goes. Feel the walls of this room – assure yourself it is real. The air can barely sustain the flame of a single candle – and these walls, built up through the centuries, are impassable to any scream.

So, begin your scream. Know we can hear every note of it. And now, as you thus call, we are casting you. We cast you as namelessness – your role is that of nothingness – a living, conscious emptiness shall be your part.

You will feel only when we turn our eyes upon you. Until then know you are but a silly void... but now I have noticed you, I have cast you, to play opposite me, at the other far end of the stage.

As We have created you, thus shall you be. And nothing else. No will nor even a whim shall obtrude from this specialised void who is you. You are as you are, for Our Purpose only. That is why We made you. And you shall never know Us, in return.

This will cause you to try to deny Us – to run away, refuse your role, try to be other than what We have designed you for.

This is the cause of all the misery in the Universe.

the dominatrix as archetype

We who harbour the strong virtue of Being-Worthy-Of-Worship know We have no choice – but to point Ourselves in one direction – away from the material grovel, We must aspire to more than our petty needs. We comprehend at last how base it is to wish to control anything – other than Ourselves, the most difficult task! As We attain self-perfection, so We as Archetypes might continue to inspire.

The Superior' nature garners great rewards and a multitude of devotees. But with these privileges comes dire Duty. We are a form of Priest – yet our methodical rites shall ever be viewed as madness. We are creators of order – discipline of the physical body being our serious tool. We are the irritating grain of sand, that the weak eye may be rubbed of sleep.

The rituals of the sadomasochist, the fetishist, even the parapath are movements of certainty in a world debased by mild relativity. We adore the Superior one; the lowly submit; imperfection abuts the Perfect; balance is restored. This is no empty worship, no dress-up game, nor a sinister 'black-magickal' manipulation. For once our preliminary groundwork is laid, in all details, with care and subtlety, the field is free to know Paradise.

The integration of sex with worship shall be salutary for the future. Tests and trials of worthiness – feats of strength – to undergo an ordeal! What bliss!

We of a certain temperament require an Ideal as the guiding force of life. Our essentially religious need for beauty and order is

Terence Sellers

pronounced; we are its slave. Let us now enter that Otherworld where Power is found; that which we love may seem to some a thing abhorrent. I love the Superior. What would be for others a danger – debasement – ruin – is for Us the possibility to know glory and perfection.

And what of the dirty workshop where Ideals are made?

And it is with her voice and her eyes alone that the ritual is elicited. Induced frenzy, flagellation, terror, contempt, hatred and the will to subjugate live in the complex of her field. Anxiety, morbid desires, the compulsion to confess, expression of irrational fear, strange wanderings are not only permitted, but invoked. All such outbursts are required for the Catharsis to flow.

The modern person certainly believes there is 'no such thing' as a true slave. The idea of such a being lives amongst them as a rejected fantasy, trails along behind them as a kind of ghost they would not have in their house. They also would fail to recognize their Superiors, much less respect them. Such stupidity continues to degrade culture, mediocritize taste, and has rendered more than one generation incapable of thought beyond their feeding and their breeding-spawning. (Democratic ideals as productive of a culture of enlightenment we must admit is *still* a failure.)

And no trace of toleration can either be found in the arena of sex. Diversity there is not well-appreciated. The interests of the 'authorities' lie in the continuing repression of sex, into the family unit: man and woman, married and breeding. Those who would not marry so will suffer rejection in society; surely a benefit to seek, in this society! Vaguely, and by rote is the mystery of sex comprehended by these bores. They fear it, would not enter in, prefer to condemn and decry what they cannot feel. Sex must be well-trimmed, behind the picket fence, and normal as determined by procreative parts. Any excess energy may seek release through socially acceptable forms of violence such as football/soccer, beating one's spouse, alcoholism, and the narcotic television.

That our favourite therapy might one day be 'legitimized' I do not hope to believe. I would say off the cuff that its adherents are well-served in staying clandestine, subject to no authority but their own.

sadomasochism for the "beginner"

We have at times had to suffer an audience with the nervous novice, the jaded thrill-seeker, and other know-nothings who entreat us to offer them instruction in 'basic' practices of sadomasochism. I here admit my failure to do so, and will not be the one to inspire the idea that anyone may blithely engage in that behaviour. Sadomasochism is not a game. The activities related to it ought never to be divorced from the reality they have symbolically grown out of. Those who would play at S&M are like those who lip-sync to a song: they may briefly involve part of their passionate bodies, but they are not bound to the Art. It is so very like the moderns to seek a pleasure without acknowledging its potential fatal effect. We are not here to entertain the bored jade in need of variation, and we will not dispense with psychology, nor philosophy, nor with the mystic strain which is no mere idyll but the crux of the hard proposition that is sadomasochist sensibility. If we did lend ourselves to a banal 'how-to', offering simple directives, formulae for scenarios, sketches of bondage positions or kinky costuming, we would be as irresponsible as a surgeon handing over his scalpel with scribbled diagram showing where to cut on the dotted line.

Those who would truly be instructed, first look to your own inclination of instinct, to garner in private study this knowledge you think you do not already possess. To delve thus into the interior reaches of true desire I warn you is a constant in the life of We Abnormals. Even well-wrought knowledge of one's proclivities today may become obsolete in first enactment. As Jung put it, "a complete emptying of the unconscious is out of the question, if only because its creative powers are continually producing new formations." The Ideal that brought one to perfect pleasure in the private study may in the Cathedral only darken the Altar. As apostates we cannot rest, spend our lives mostly unecstatic, hacking out beloved Approximations from what drifts our way.

Anyone who is set upon enjoying a Master-slave or Mistress-slave relationship must acknowledge they are tapping into a vein of primitive and explosive energy – what Freud termed a 'death-instinct', a theory much maligned. This instinct we might liken to a rapacious Will-To-Power, that vaunts itself and its needs above those of any other. In the sadomasochist this instinct is linked up with the libido, its energy thereby becoming a rapacious thing, amoral, satanic.

It is usually suppressed by cultural demands, and is the psychic current for creativity when sublimated.

To assume the role of Superior Mistress-Master has far-reaching, transformative, and at times highly disturbing, consequences. The modern popularity of sadomasochist iconography in our *fin-de-siècle* does not signify that it is just another happy facet of sexual expression. S&M sex is not some other flavour, licorice instead of vanilla. It is a symptom of the profound dissociation between the body and what lives sensitively within, requiring love and nurture. Sadomasochism proves that there might be no chasm between the perverse imperatives of a Will-To-Power, and the capacity to love and be loved – as there ought to be. That there are pleasures to be had in our cold realm does not soften, or justify the reality that we of sadomasochistic bent suffer from *a special anaesthesia of feeling*. Certainly, when the dead senses are violently reawakened through the needed, severe methods, the triumphal *jouissance* can be so tempestuous as to be called 'better' than normal sex – hence the touting by some devotees that our pleasure is a *superior* one. No – it is simply much more *difficult* to achieve.

Everyone has within them some inclination to either dominate his fellow-man, or to serve him. This does not however mean that 'everyone is a sadomasochist'. One only achieves that distinction when active aggression, or pliant submissiveness or a combination of the two is necessary to successful sexual release. The door into this pleasure is fantasy, whose material is wrought from trauma. The spectrum of sadomasochism opens at one end with sexual intercourse, "the normal sex impulse is always bound to a more or less brutal element", as Stekel found – that *more* in his statement pointing to the closure of the spectrum, towards the psychotic who must mutilate and shed blood to gain orgasm. One may cultivate pleasurable fantasies of subjugating the object of one's desires, or of suffering the control of a fascinating conqueror. But how these fantasies will obtrude into reality as an activity – for in some way *they must* – is a matter *of serious and cautious consideration.* Such thoughts and fantasies do not arise without reason – and as they are more or less urgent, *they require resolution.* They may serve merely to enhance the normal sex act, i.e. loving intercourse between same or opposite sex. Or they may obsess one to the point of nightmare, to feelings of demonic possession, undermining the ego-controls so that the constraint of their being criminal cannot halt an attack upon a child or other truly helpless being. It is to the work of those who, without injuring others or themselves, can aid in the expression of potentially fatal ideas, that I address myself – and it is their work – my work – that I here reveal – that middle, creative field of psychodramatic action, as wrought in the Theatrical Dungeon: our modern Purgatory of transgression and trial, judgement and punishment.

Now distinguish between our Know-Nothing applicants: the thrill-seeker who is merely bored with sex as he knows it deserves no further consideration; but the poor nervous novice who is sincerely in need of fulfilment, faces a first great difficulty in knowing whom to trust with his terrified confession. He does not know enough to even judge if a Master-Mistress is a true one. Even as *We* evolve in self-knowledge, this task becomes no easier. Though in large metropolitan areas one will find social-clubs set up for like-minded perverts to meet, some find such gatherings a special kind of torment. The highly individualised nature of one's S&M complex almost invariably precludes its finding satisfaction in vulgar cocktail-party *milieux*, open to the public and overrun with exhibitionists, whom are seen to be quite happy there. Not only do I resent being made their voyeur, the debasement inherent in attending such routs is not to be tolerated, as one is set upon by a pack of naked fools or overhung by drunken bullies. Too, there is the danger of meeting up with your executioner. I was made party once to certain information, that so many dead men, left in bloodied bondage, had last been seen trolling at a notorious gay leather-bar, that Manhattan detectives had to themselves become regulars and cruise its pungent precincts undercover. Masochists are earnestly enjoined to fail to bring home the handsome passing stranger – even should he command you to.

Many male masochists receive their initiation into S&M rite from the hands of the Dominatrix, or professional female sadist. In this way they may exert some initial control over their experience, which is advisable. They do arrive as strangers at the shores of an unknown. To submit within the confines of an hour's time, with perhaps not fullest submission, enables him to apprise himself of The Mistress' experience and style, and whether she may be relied upon to care about him at all. If the first scene is satisfactory to both, a relationship can be developed where the limits of the masochist/submissive may be expanded or refined. He may wish to learn what pleases her, too, and mould himself to serve her pleasure. In this earliest relation to the slave – of service – there is no submission for the Mistress, as some may snigger. Without these accommodating trials, grievous psychic error or physical injury could be the result. The Dominatrix as psychologist, therapist, nurse and business-woman will manifest a high level of responsible behaviour towards the slave. She understands the experience he is to have may mark him indelibly, and will not wish to damage further an already volatile, uneasy psyche. Under these restraints, determined to a practical degree by the maintaining of 'the business', she will observe safe and conscientious methods. Though a professional Mistress may not be one's ultimate and loving ideal, she provides a hygienic service and the not-to-be-maligned opportunity to further one's private self-study.

Let us imagine now that you are of a submissive nature, and are involved in a so-called normal relationship. You have not revealed your bent to your chosen partner, but one reason that you became involved at all is that you believe your beloved to harbour the rare seed of the Mistress-Master.

You have considered a hundred times in a hundred ways how you might draw this relationship into the theatre of your perversity. Your understanding of the mechanics of sadomasochism now forces you to realize that *you* must take the initiative if anything is to occur. Much as you may loathe it, you shall one evening take on the role of the dominant! But as your favoured position is the bottom, you will thereafter almost immediately enjoin your lover to do to you as you had done. Do not overdo this exercise! Terrorizing your partner by strange and insistent demands is not only improperly submissive, but clumsy. By degrees you will discover how much or little of such activities they will tolerate. We do not want all cards out on the table.

If you are fortunate, and certain roles develop between you, still continue with that oscillation of dominant with submissive. For if you rush too eagerly into your submissive role, not to be budged from it, your less knowing partner will not be granted the leisure to peruse the elements of a pleasure you pray they will concatenate.

It is no small matter to introduce the strictures of dominance and submission into a relationship. Though I have been able to train both men and women to be my slaves, I have not had much success in finding one who could grant me the pleasure of deep submission. The level of sophistication, technical and psychic, I have attained through the ardent practice of years does make it close to impossible to meet my match and equal Master-Mistress. On two occasions I attempted to seductively train and sensitize my lovers to dominate me as I require. In the exercise of this rare privilege of ruling me, both behaved badly under the supersensual thrall of what they suddenly, strangely considered absolute ownership. (Among professionals, such mania is termed 'New Mistress Syndrome', manifesting as the inability to stop ruling: constant bossing, bitching and carrying on in ways not in the least charming outside the Theatre.) If I enjoyed a certain physical strenuousness, or some symbolic humiliation in the *boudoir*, it did not follow that verbal abuse, public humiliation or emotional manipulation would be as passionately embraced. Of course I cannot utterly castigate those two souls I would have made Masters. Based on the evidence of the bedroom, they felt they had the right to torment me anew and interestingly. For some reason, both were entranced by the idea of putting me on some kind of display, to perform for them before a crowd. This I found noxious, but they did not care. Their intoxication in the Rule had put them out of their heads in my regard. My refusal to submit brought rage and rejection, which did of course not seduce me further. All pleasure was destroyed in the sad undoing.

The bleeding over from the physical sadism into an emotional sadism I would say is the greatest argument against the introduction of S&M 'games' into your love-making. It is logical: once your fiancée has seen you creeping, wagging your tail and begging, not to mention barking, or worrying your shoe, how will she love you in the same way? If she is not instantly filled with contempt, she will certainly pity you. "Why are you doing that: DO YOU HAVE TO DO THAT?" Well, yes.

If their love is truly unconditional, and they are enough enlightened to hear in your barks the happy catharsis, you may be the lucky dog who wears the gilded leash, never to fear you may be turned outdoors to scrabble gutter-wise with the mutts.

There is a cliché that a good Dominant ought to know that other side; and as much as We hate to admit to our past as slaves, We owe much of our present power to some long ago Initiator. Early in my life as a Dominatrix I found that to oscillate between the two roles was essential in order to maintain a certain level of mental stability. The constant of being worshipped does induce a kind of insanity, in which one can believe that one is infallible. To truly be convinced that "Nothing I do is wrong!", as someone once shouted at me in a restaurant, is all the more reason for them to pick up the check. Yes, whatever you say – but pay.

The determination of the Mistress-Master to keep sensitized may be illustrated by Mistress Ava Beaumont, who once offered me much in the way of wise instruction. I then thought her slightly mad to act as she did on this one occasion, but I now comprehend how she required some strict reminders to assure her continuing efficacy as a working Dominatrix with some species of soul.

The place where she and I had our employ was owned by a man who rather voyeuristically enjoyed a 'possession' of us, but had enough to occupy himself with in a number of 'straight houses', so that he left us to work alone. But about once a month, he would take us shopping, at the warehouse of a large S&M supply. We would run through the place, taking what we wanted in the way of new and advanced torture equipment, amongst other delicate devices. Then, when Ava and I got back to our Dungeon, she would have me try out every instrument upon her. We did not assume dominant or submissive roles, though I felt strangely submissive to her as she insisted I truly hit her with the fresh bull-whip. I balked at turning on the electro-prod, a mild shocking-device, but she urged me, gibing, "Don't you want to feel it too?" I was yet inexperienced, and too obsessed with my dominant persona to let it drop so far, but I admired her willingness to know every sensation that she was to later artfully inflict upon our clients. I was thus introduced to one of the hygienic methods to be employed by the correct sadist.

This is not to say that one must be willing to suffer everything, or anything your slave will endure. Obviously certain refinements of penis-torture cannot be known by the female sex. (This making our own sex our own best tormentors.) If we can feel no slight reverberation of their pain within ourselves, we cannot fully control what they will feel. Trust can only grow, and submission be assured, if you are able to relent the pain at that instant *before* they cry for mercy. Eyes will shine with wonder and respect at your sensitive perception ...

The experienced Master-Mistress can often 'read' a slave, determine as by instinct what he or she may desire. After five years, when my practice was wide and had refined itself, I began to notice not only an increase in this intuition, but an unusual, developing faculty. When the slave knelt before me, in first submission, I not only anticipated what the fantasy would be, but I felt on my own body where he needed the pain. I experienced it as an itching, or tingling. More than once I developed scenarios that too closely approximated early trauma. I did cause some fear, "Who told you? How did you know ... do you know her?" as I spoke of a relative, ex-lover, even once or twice 'guessing' the woman's name. Then the 'shadow pains' began: as I struck or tortured, or even spoke a cruel word, I felt on my own body a reverberation of the pain they were feeling. Perhaps the strangest thing in this is that it took five years to happen. This deadness overcome reminds me of a statement taken from one of the Manson women: she told police that when she drove the knife into the body of her victim, she felt as though she were stabbing herself.

I became convinced of my transparency one evening when I had enforced bondage upon an aficionado who was paying for the privilege of staying tied up all night. I had of course taken a great deal of time to insure that no knot was too tight, no angle of limb too awkward to withstand the hours he was to remain restrained. I was however a bit uneasy as I turned out the lights and locked the door. I was sound asleep at seven a.m. when I was awakened by a terrific cramp down the whole left side of my body. I was so numb I could barely walk to the bathroom, and my thoughts seemed centred upon the slave. How was he? I had to go and see, dressed, and achieved the Dungeon door. As I came in he called out in distress. As he had slept he had twisted sideways, and lay with his full weight on his left side. His cramped and painful wrist as well reflected upon my own weakened hand. This faculty to shadow the pain of others I have used to inform myself of physical needs, psychic disturbance, and the levels of tolerance for pain, which at times is mysteriously fluxuant. This psychism also manifests as receptive telepathy, so we know as a certainty when a special slave is to call, or appear, these 'psychic sex slaves' being of course favourite devotees.

The aspirant to a position of Master or Mistress – or the brave adept who would be professional Slave, for that matter – should place themselves early on under the rule of an excellent Tutor. You will of course know what your own proclivities are; but more than attaining to your private satisfaction will your task be to investigate and draw out in others whatever their own bent might be. Every client, submissive or dominant, should be treated as a special case, carefully interviewed and handled individually. Unusual physical conditions, unstable psychic states, emotional flaccidity or over-responsiveness will be looked for in the in-depth interview. As their self-acceptance, as well, of their parapathy is great or nil, you will remark on the varieties of private evolution.

There ought never to be, for the conscientious Operator, something known as a 'standard session'. This modern marketing of an essentially psychological service, under wholesale conditions of assumed uniformity is a dangerous abuse in the profession. You may mark the know-nothing thrill-seeker by his question: "What do you usually do?" One may of course be in a certain mood that day – wishing only for a decent foot-massage, so admitting only that devotee. What we 'usually do' is dominate, but rarely in the same way... the Whim is often the Will.

So ought the aspirant Practitioner to stand first in the way of considering their Ideals: what to them Superiority means; to become familiar with the Ethics of control; to research the literature; to listen to and learn from the subjects who offer themselves up for study; to practice knots, polish up the diction, attend to wardrobe, and worry less at first about technique than the development of a Correct consciousness.

We will insist again that the nervous novice be cautious in his selection of his Superior. It may seem rude, or ironic to advise the slave to examine Us for defects, prior to his kneeling. But the dangers inherent in submission will soon be forgotten in an early, wild subjection. As repression breaks down, over you rushes exhilarated relief. The probability of obsession can be high, and consequences fatal. When shame comes to you – and it will – let it wash your eyes quite clear. See yourself, do not forget anything, for one of the best effects of your passionate debasement should be an attachment that will ultimately aid you in the acceptance of your desires.

On the other side, the new Mistress-Master cannot expect from their subjects perfect submission at all times. Masochists, submissives and other menials tend to give their all, and immediately, and also to pretend they are. You will hear their anthem-cries of "Anything", which very often means nothing at all. Demand a total submission and end up with crumbs and a crust. "Anything!" – if it were only so. For that positive, cathartic breakthrough that is the sadomasochist's ecstasy, slave and Superior must each in their own way *lose control*. The slave does this of course through the door of fantasy, but what We as aspirants to the ultimate Will seek is that one terrifying second, when We know We may truly do ANYTHING We want ... with our willing subjects.

... and as We come to the end of the pain, as We draw the rein in on the tormenting hand, We pause – pause in that exalted instant – yes let us add just one more drop of poison – and in those final cries we know our satisfaction: we have given up control at the height of control – we have let them live. So we set them free, to torture them another day.

For The 'Beginner': Small Additional Warning Against The Amateur Dominatrix And The Drug-Addict 'Superior'

As the true Superior is to the devoted slave, so are heroin and cocaine to the addict Master-Mistress. We understand how awful it is for the slave to have to correct Us; the proper etiquette of address will aid him or her in this trial. Maintain your submissiveness, even if crying inside – or seething. If depressing revelations of unworthiness overwhelm you whilst in bondage, or some other equally helpless, subject state, do not risk offending your Overlord in his or her delirium. Puffed up with a crude and specious power, the addict Master-Mistress will take your resistance as a challenge, a threat to their ego. They must be viewed as being out of control. And it is just at that challenged moment, when their Will is most urgently required, when they could fight off the drug's false exaltations, that the Will is utterly paralysed, stupid in the clutch of the drug. You might then find yourself more tightly bound, gagged, beaten and tormented yet more cruelly – for which you would have no-one but yourself to blame, as you probably offered an incorrect resistance.

"Please, dear Master-Mistress, I want to submit to you completely, but I feel I cannot please you today ... I have many worries ... I feel weak ..." that is, do blame yourself as an imperfect subject for control and make your escape.

Abstention from the use of addicting drugs throughout the session is an imperative. You do not require *two* extreme submissions in your life. Should these substances be proffered by your so-called Superior, refuse with good grace and quit their precincts forever. Admix your worship with these lees of Death, and your submission will end as a satanic footnote we will not wish to read.

impoverishment in modern life due to an absence of the serving classes

One of the classical relationships of humanity that cannot be eradicated (no matter though modern prejudice will try) is that the mass of the human race shall ever be in service to small, elite coteries within it. We state here once and for all that the democratic 'ideal' (that all might be equal under God) is a naive, almost inane fantasy. The democratic delusion has usurped the ideal of Divine Right – which it would do well for all to reassume: that there is an Order in Nature – a natural law – that we mere species cannot controvert – that Some within the species are superior to others – and that these *should* rule the masses! Why *ought* there be any escape from this natural hierarchy, of the best atop the better above the good – and the worst held in subjection to all? The inability to respect and honour the Best, to try to drag everyone down to some wretched middle ground where all can agree (and the idiots will never agree with the intelligent) has brought this society into a ridiculous disorder, marked by the endemic *reversal of all values.* What the stupidest desire – what the dullest admire – what the greediest require – have become the standards under which we all have suffered *too long.* It ought *by now* to be obvious to any person of sensibility that this fantasy has been a source of degeneration on every social level.

> *Where the herd animal is irradiated by the glory of*
> *the purest virtue, the exceptional man must have*

been devalued into an evil.[1]

This fantasy exists in education, with a significant lowering of all standards, so that teenagers are 'graduated' still not knowing how to read. It penetrates the institution of marriage, so that divorce is almost the logical result. Within the engine of politics we have no rule by the best, but by a caste of the cynically ambitious. It has poisoned the arts so that we have a lurid 'mass culture', appealing not to reason, the sense of beauty, or the intellect but to atavistic lusts. Because the masses are pandered to, not put under any ideals and disciplined thereby, no-one knows their place. *Yet place we all must have – and it shall ever be for Some Few to determine what your place shall be!*

Few have been able to countenance even the codicil that every man, *and woman*, might be somehow equal to every other man *and woman* ... to assent to every levelling permutation within *that* squared equation alone is an exhausting impossibility for *all* parties involved ... and thus is a war that shall eternally rage. Is not the very phrase *created equal* clumsy and unlovely? Could the Masons who inscribed the fateful parchment have really meant that such a truth could ever be self-evident? These we hold self-evident in our turn: *the only distinctions that shall be recognized are those of the soul – of incorruptible integrity – of cultivated intellect – of strong principle and usefulness – of fidelity in seeking for truth.*[2] Our trial under this 'democratic' sentence has served one purpose – it has proved to We who must Rule that we must never again abjure our Ascension!

It shall here be qualified that the author is no partisan of that vulgar hierarchy that would designate one race, creed, sex, financial status or social position as the worthy one to kneel before. It might happen that We of the Elect may acquire an exalted place in society, but this has nothing to do with 'high' society or any such

---

[1] Nietzsche, *Ecce Homo*, 'Why I Am Destiny'.

[2] Paraphrase, Channing, Wm. E., *On The Elevation Of The Labouring Classes* (1840)

Terence Sellers

conventional position of privilege. For We are concerned here with only one imperative – whether one has the psychic predisposition towards the Rule, and can accept every responsibility that entails upon that Rule. This is nothing conferred or awarded, but is as a stratum of the character, made up both of perfected qualities and strange fault-lines that lend it power. Into the halo of its 'charisma' we are drawn to worship. Even within a fanatic's basement a twisted beauty compels. In orbit around the Superior we may identify its brotherhood – its predetermined Subject – Those Who Would Be Ruled. The generations of enlightened masters and their servants-in-place have died out – but they might come to be again. There are too many people, too great a 'mass', for everyone to be in wretched individuation. There is nothing essentially degrading in being a servant, unless one's master be a degraded animal, which has been the case where privilege was measured by one's quantity of cash-money. Therefore it is now essential to clarify in one's mind the concept of a Divine Right – that is, that We who hold power and who Rule must invest ourselves thoroughly in a prayer – yes, a prayer! – to that Spirit who is more perfected than we, upon whom we (shall eternally) model ourselves. We make it our daily trial to conceive of this Spirit, to worship it, above any egoistic imperatives, and measure ourselves as ever falling short of it.

There is little respect for, and hardly a belief in the ideal of a Willing Servant. A fantasy that most of us will never realize is to be able to pursue our lives in a world where we can absolutely count upon the good-will of others. Instead of a peasantry, attached indian-like to the land and versed in that valuable knowledge, we have herds of transient 'workers'. There is barely a class of hardy people for hire. The greater sense of community amongst their own kind, and of order thereby in the world at large, was granted, we see now, as a kind of privilege to the land-attached 'slave', or to the servant taken into an aristocratic family. The modern 'worker' is a degenerate of the species, in attitude alternating between contempt and depression. They fill mere slots in the impersonal engines of industry, working for money only. They suffer this wage-slavery badly, as they ought. Such workers have not the faintest love for the 'order' they have been hired into, a faceless, often irresponsible corporation. This gross 'mass-ification' of industry subjects us all to a shocking lack of service, whether it be a cup of coffee served, or a car delivered. Meet a stare of shock, then derision, should you require these workers to do their job – much less ask them for any special attention. It is scarcely their fault, however – for the masses do make a very bad Master.

One defining quality of the true servant and submissive is their psychic readiness to attach themselves to, admire, and take part in all things that relate to the One whom the worshipper has himself, freely, recognized and valued as greater than him or herself. In the dominating personality of the natural Ruler, there is the predisposition to accept all the good things of life – including the efforts of others – as something of their own. This may include those material 'good things', or may mean they only profess to attain the privileged precincts of high intellect, which will take its natural advantage. Both servant and Master thus will seem almost magically gifted in creating their own unique theatre of influence, where only suchlike minds may convene, wherein the furnishings will be agreeable. It does happen, almost inadvertently it may seem, that the Dominator naturally takes control of the lives, and destinies of others; they become in their way an influence for prosperity. To thus receive service from those who will automatically benefit from this ascendancy is only the just due of these Intellects. To be able to serve such as They for the servant becomes a spiritual necessity, feels like a destiny, and is undeniably one of the greatest pleasures known to man.

One may still experience in the finest restaurants and in first-class hotels forms of high-service that have become almost anachronistic. We may not exact these services as a right we must enjoy, but we must pay for them. The degrading transactions that cash-money imposes leaves those of us without excessive means unfairly without the best of service. Peasantry that occasionally wander into such fine establishments will be appropriately intimidated by the grandeur of the servants there.

To be in possession of an excellent Master or Mistress was once a source not only of good fortune and security, but of high honour and happiness. Now the need for cash-money in nearly every exchange of life makes it impossible for the subservient nature to lend itself to personal service to one they may deem worthy of their services. Again, the Ruler without excessive means will find it difficult to maintain a staff of the deserving, unless this staff work elsewhere to help support the endeavour. Because of the ridiculous modern prejudice for the independent existence, the function of manservant and lady-companion has been rendered an impossibility, in an awful world where cash rules. To the true servant, cash can only be a gift. 'Wages' are an insult to his position in life – for he shares in the life of his Master and Mistress.

The enlightened slaver always assures him or herself of a proper enslavement by considering both the quality of the servile temperament, and the depth of the submissive character. It is the Master-Mistress' responsibility to properly position the slave in a role consonant with his talents. There are thousands living now in our unpleasant era who have been forced into an ungratifying independence, who would like it well if they might lose their useless freedom and live in intimate attachment to a great Mistress-Master. To be part of a great estate, of a large and well-ordered household that is sufficient unto its own self (with grounds, farm-industry, trade, and private army) because of the well-regulated and concerted efforts of all who have the privilege to live there – is again an ideal that few will ever realize in our degenerated society. The typical 18th Century aristocratic European household could not respect itself if it employed less than two hundred servants in town alone. Imagine the translation of these standards into our modern times. Each servant was fed, clothed, and housed, and as well held a relatively high position in society – with no vulgar 'wages' ever exchanging hands. In our pathetically 'progressive' era there are actually laws of employment to prevent the erection of such an establishment. On the same note, we also consider it patently unfair that free men no longer have the option of selling themselves into slavery (though I am sure some divorced husbands would cry out that alimony is just such a bondage). We pretend that one human being might not own another – yet the attachments that cash-money impose create more afflictions than any ownership of flesh by flesh ever did. If some of us within these human ranks might accept and live by the strict truth that no-one can possibly be equal to another, why should the dreadful egalitarians deny us our pursuit of happiness?

To conclude, I return to that tediously empty, if not utterly stupid atmosphere of our modern world. To think we might be 'created equal' is hardly any more a potent notion. The strange social acceptability of sadomasochism reflects a reaction in our time against such false and levelling concepts. Sadomasochism is certainly an atavism, a throwback to an earlier level of human development. Earlier, perhaps – but not less evolved. Through its practices *we restore the lost pleasure in hierarchy.* Through a sexual will, we revert to the primitive *and true* – through ritual psychodrama, we realize once more (for however brief and ecstatic moments) that ancient right of one to be atop the other! By these arcane means the slave too may perform once again his ancient, sacred duty to Obey. The assumption of these hierarchies recreates us strong, imperial and whole – whether we are Master-Mistress or subject.

Outside the flat plateau of modern democracy, our challenge is to realize a true psychic Superiority – or to become a heart of Devotion. Both shall be ruled by a divinely righteous Will. *We determine to make this no fantasy.*

Terence Sellers

towards a school of manners

I once possessed a friend who was an adept in the art of sadistic variation, and I knew the pleasure of spending some time with him in a remote abode. His very proper upbringing did on occasion exert some strain upon his Nature; his best cruel ideals he often revealed only to me. While he could appear congenial, charming, and correctly sociable, in truth he often loathed the diddling annoying niceties demanded by convention, particularly as a veritable slough of visitors soon descended upon us in our obscure retreat. After yet another afternoon lost to Art, wasted in entertaining the idle, hungry and unannounced, he appealed to me to erect some barrier between himself and the constant stream of callers. He knew he could be assured that I, who am by Nature unmoved by imperatives to the norm, would devise the clever diverting artifice, to arrest and subdue the gruesome importunities of those who believe that persons buried in the deep sticks must be (I shudder) *lonely* ... We both wished for nothing more than peace and quiet, and while his style might continue to assert that society was more than welcome, to the restrictions of my tyranny he could 'sadly' point as *determining* – and with a hurried whisper aside that he feared my *temper* should he *dare* controvert me. Thus we enjoyed the fruits of my 'ill-bred' violence, that is to say, we were *left alone*, in splendid solitude, upon the posting in the vestibule of the following 'House Rules':

THE HELL HOTEL SCHOOL OF MANNERS

Upon entering these estates, all guests become Students, subject to the Rule of the Headmaster and Headmistress. Transgressions from Manner is subject to Demerit. Carry your Demerit Card with you at all times. Demerits are determined by the Whim of the Headmaster and/or the Headmistress.

<u>List Of Transgressions</u>

1. Rudeness. Boorishness. Sheer stupidity.
2. Conversational Error: to Wit, the lack of it; dull subject matter; the lengthy recounting of dreams; other rambling nonsense; poor elocution; loud and vulgar delivery; Philistine philosophies. Impingement upon forbidden topics will be subject to multiple Demerits. Forbidden topics subject to the Whim of the Headmaster and Headmistress.
3. Unattractive forms of sexual repression, or expression, e.g. homophobias, or scatological exhibitionism.
4. Failure to continually express the required forms of obeisance, respect, or worship proper to your grade-level towards the Headmaster or Headmistress.
5. Failure in wardrobe.
6. Being fat and unconcernedly pig-like.
7. Failure in absolute punctuality.
8. Gross table manners; restaurant *faux-pas.*
9. Manifesting the inability to understand the subjects *proper to your grade-level.* Unimproved performance will result in furthering showering of Demerits, and Demotion to yet lower levels. Continuing failure in this regard will result in automatic Expulsion.
10. Enshrined mediocrity will be tolerated for the length of three seconds. Thereupon will follow a showering of Demerits, and compulsory blasphemy from all Students.
11. Additional Transgressions will be daily invented and imposed. All Students of the School are totally responsible for keeping up with the latest Diatribe. Ignorance of the Whim is no excuse for disobeying the Whim!

I received my friend's private accolades at the pertinacity of these Impositions. Those of our visitors who were able to read and comprehend the Truth of the Manner instantly requested their Demerit Cards. Those unable to read or absorb the Logic of the Arcana were left to their fate, whining and bickering amongst themselves against the elephantine snobbery we only enjoyed: for

---

in that they did indeed manifest an inability to understand a subject proper to their grade-level, and thus to their appropriately lower class in our School were they speedily demoted.

PART TWO

THE CASE HISTORIES OF DOCTOR A. STERN

(or)
"A Compleat Masochist"

the use of 'it'

In dialogue with slaves, an important 'reality' to emphasize is that they are merely things: nameless, faceless, lumps of dough to be moulded into anything and acted upon in any way. He is a mechanism without personal identity: 'not human'. No will is ever allowed to be made manifest, nor should they ever speak.

Two Superior Beings discuss the traits of the Thing at hand.

X: I have found it to be quite useful.
X2:   You wouldn't know that from looking at it.
-x: ....
X: To own one of these types of vacuum appliances saves a great deal on the electric bill.
X2:   But can it really suck up everything? It looks weak.
X: Everything.
X2:   Every grain of dirt, every speck of dust, every hair? It gets up everything?
-x: ....
X: If it doesn't, we merely run it through the house again.
X2:   My feet are killing me. Where's the footstool?
-x hurries to serve this function.
X2:   Delightful. Aah. I'd like to have one of these for my home.
X: I'd lend you mine, but they break so easily.
X2:   Yes, and I am quite hard on appliances. I don't know my own strength – I get angry and they start to malfunction.
X: You mean they start to malfunction and you get angry.
X2:   That too. I've broken quite a few.
X: I rather enjoy breaking them. Then I can get new ones.
-x: ....

X2:   I think it looked at you.

X: Just as I was about to say that this one hadn't malfunctioned yet. Advanced Footstool!

-x rolls over on his back and applies his hands vigorously to the feet of X2.

X: See, when you turn it over, it vibrates and your feet can experience delightful massage.

X2:   Aah, very nice. Where could I get one like it?

X: I'm having it cloned; I'll send you one at Xmas.

-x: ....

X2:   How curious. Your appliance has a depressed look.

X: You're stepping on it too hard. I told you they were breakable.

X2:   It's slowing down ... is it broken already?

X: It may need gas. (*Swipes -x smartly with a crop.*) So, it wishes to be only *my* piece of property. How poor I'd be, if that were so! Remember, even if you are not to be cloned, you can always be replaced!

-x: ....

X2:   Where do you get replacements? I don't want a clone of this one. I want a young, slender blonde one.

X: Replacements can be found just about anywhere. You just have to know how to demand one.

who is always correct?

You would like to believe that you possess some control over your life. You prefer to think that you are quite responsible for the order and disorder that surrounds you. Such illusions will pacify. But in truth what do you know – anything? What of these influences at work ever upon you? What of the earthquake in China a hundred years ago, that even now resonates within your body? How do you know it is not so? Do you exist at all? You are subject, without wanting or willing it so, to every kind of sound, vision, thought, view, vibration, rainstorm that ever was, or ever shall be. And it is (I know) an even more noxious thought to you that every fact and facet of your life has been decided upon in advance – perhaps in advance of your conception, and birth. Your perversities certainly were so determined, and even your rebellion against this idea. Too your hard-wrought genius – all. While even the most sheepish amongst you will firmly state he must graze for grass only upon his chosen hill, I have no such hungers. My peculiar combination of temperament and tastes easily accepts the idea of a predetermined destiny. Odd is it not, in such a one you might well think would be overweeningly convinced of free-will and a private, powerful control? And neither can I know where my reach within the world extends or ends, nor, most saliently, how my influence over another human being may work, for good or ill, if at all. That some good gestures have generated evil, that cruelty and indifference may do good, are but more arguments pleasing to my whim to know the Deterministic Ineffable.

In a predetermined universe I know myself as already as perfect as I shall ever be. My conviction of my own innate perfection, the direction this consciousness turns me in, sets me far apart from you striving free-willers, always in the agony of attainment. I have attained – and it had nothing to do with me.

You who insist most wildly upon your individual, freely-willed grasp – you are anxious! Go on building your private metaphysic, insist that Order is your subjective doctrine. You are nothing! For within you I see there still must be Someone – Who Is Always Correct! The Ideal of the Superior Being rises to accede to your needful gaze. Can you be reminded that this 'Greater' is ever a fantasy? May you go insane under the imperative of a Perfection never to be realized. Perhaps that may draw you further on towards your own.

Needless to say the attempt to be for all of you a Perfection is a thing I will not hazard. You seekers shall find me out, to rest in the shade of my pure conviction of Beauty and Strength. These virtues have little to do with pleasingness, and even less with self-satisfaction. I am bound by Divine Right to be utterly what I am and no more. I am grateful to be thus only slightly a cripple. My dread predetermination may not be pretty, but it is my only story.

Would you attain to True Submission? Would you know and love a One Who Is Always Correct? Feel and know Void in yourself, that place where you know you have no control. Fill it with your burning passion, whatever that might be, no matter the horror of that hunger. Feed its flames, and your face to the flames. For you to feel how faceless you are is our blessing upon you.

Burn, and reflect; burn and reflect. Turn your eyes now again upon the Superior: you may be gazing upon a massy, overwrought, bloated ego – but such as They are Certain, while you shall remain eternally at odds. Though your Superior may yet prove unworshippable, still they are Gods and you are not.

<u>Who Is Always Correct? Dialogue Between Mistress Helga And Slave Jeffrey</u>

Through the exquisite improvisational talent of Mistress Helga of Manhattan we were able, in a moment of eavesdropping, to derive this dialogue. She as the forever Unknown Knower both crushes and exalts the blank thing that is Jeffrey.

Slave is discovered kneeling before the throne. Helga takes her place thereupon.

Mistress Helga: Who is right?
Slave Jeffrey: (No response)
Mistress Helga: Who is Always Right?
Slave Jeffrey: (No response)
Mistress Helga: Who-Is-Always-Correct?
Slave Jeffrey: You are, Mistress – you are.
Mistress Helga: And who Knows you, Slave?
Slave Jeffrey: (No response)
Mistress Helga: Slave – who Knows you – so well?
Slave Jeffrey: Mistress you do, you Know me, you own me as your private property.

Mistress takes a turn around the room, away from the Slave, proprietorially touching objects, moving a chair, gazing at herself in the mirror.

Mistress Helga: I'll be living in this house for the rest of my life. I'll be right here, in your neighbourhood, right across the street from you. I'm never going to move away, and neither are you. I'll be living across the street from you for the rest of your life.
Slave Jeffrey: Yes Mistress. Let me serve you – forever.
Mistress Helga: You must have done something right – to be my slave.
Slave Jeffrey: I am grateful Mistress.
Mistress Helga: But don't be quick to assume that you hold any position here – that you're anything, in this house.
Slave Jeffrey: No Mistress.
Mistress Helga: You must still strive.

Slave Jeffrey: Always Mistress.

Mistress Helga: Even on a day when you might seem perfect, there will always be the next day, when you will be in error again.

Slave Jeffrey: I will try to be perfect.

Mistress Helga: You will never move away from here.

Slave Jeffrey: (No response)

Mistress Helga: You'll serve me for the rest of your life. I keep my slaves forever.

Slave Jeffrey: (No response)

Mistress Helga: I keep my slaves forever.

Slave Jeffrey: Thank you Mistress, thank you, keep me forever as your private property.

Mistress snarls as Slave begins to touch his private parts; demands he hold out his open palms which she strikes across with a cane.

Mistress Helga: That too is part of my property. You're not to put your hands on it without my permission. Is that understood?

Slave Jeffrey: (Being struck) O please no, no, no ...

Mistress Helga: No? Did I hear – NO? How could that be? How could it be – NO?!

Slave Jeffrey: I'm sorry I ...

Mistress Helga: WASN'T THINKING? How could you possibly, how could you ever think, to say to me NO ... are you saying ... could you possibly be thinking – that I don't know what I'm doing?

Slave Jeffrey: On, no Mistress ... never.

Mistress Helga: No, I think that's it. I think you were trying to tell me – that I was WRONG! Wrong! Imagine – me, being wrong?

Slave Jeffrey: No, never, Mistress, you could never be wrong.

Mistress Helga: Am I not Always Right? Is not everything I do flawless, without error?

Am I not Always Correct?

Slave Jeffrey is coming in for a round of serious discipline.

Mistress Helga: You see, Jeffrey, I Know you so well. I Know you much better than you know yourself. I Knew what you were thinking, even when you didn't.

Slave Jeffrey: I was wrong, I am the wrong one. I'm sorry, sorry,

sorry.

Mistress Helga: You're not sorry. I Know when you're sorry. And you're not sorry. You're not sorry yet.

The punishment continues.

Slave Jeffrey: I swear to the Goddess I'm sorry, I'll never think bad thoughts again, I'll never do anything wrong again.
Mistress Helga: I Know you, Jeffrey. You're not sorry yet.
Slave Jeffrey: I AM!
Mistress Helga: Contradicting me again?

Slave squirms in despair under the impossible restraint, trying to think his way out of the trap. If he says he is sorry before she thinks he is, he will again be guilty, and the punishment will go on.

Slave Jeffrey: I'll do anything... anything you say. Just tell me what to do.
Mistress Helga: Well, the neighbours will be coming over. All the ladies of the neighbourhood. On his knees will be Jeffrey. I think the ladies should know what's in their own neighbourhood, don't you Jeffrey.
Slave Jeffrey: Yes, I'll do anything. You know best.
Mistress Helga: Yes. Well then, let's practice your presentation. We'll practice what you're going to say to the ladies of the neighbourhood.
Slave Jeffrey: Yes Mistress.

Mistress Helga places her Slave before the mirror and renders him kneeling.

Mistress Helga: What colour are your eyes, Jeffrey?
Slave Jeffrey: (No response)
Mistress Helga: Hmm. Jeffrey? What colour are your eyes?
Slave Jeffrey: (No response)
Mistress Helga: I asked you – what colour are your eyes?
Slave Jeffrey: My eyes are blue.
Mistress Helga: Let's see. Jeffrey – your eyes are brown.
Slave Jeffrey: Brown.

Mistress Helga:	Yes – your eyes are brown – fool!
Slave Jeffrey:	My eyes are brown.
Mistress Helga:	Once again, trying to contradict me.
Slave Jeffrey:	No ... I mean yes, I tried to contradict you.
Mistress Helga:	Your eyes are brown Jeffrey. Anyone can see that.
Slave Jeffrey:	I can see that, yes. My eyes are brown.
Mistress Helga:	You see, I Know you. I Know you so well, so much better than you know yourself.
Slave Jeffrey:	You Know everything. May I touch myself?
Mistress Helga:	You may ... What colour are your eyes, Jeffrey?
Slave Jeffrey:	(No response)
Mistress Helga:	Jeffrey, what colour are your eyes?
Slave Jeffrey:	(No response)
Mistress Helga:	Who is Always Correct? Who Knows you through and through?
Slave Jeffrey:	You are. You do, my eyes are brown.
Mistress Helga:	Fool. Your eyes are blue.

Slave achieves his ultimate pleasure upon this final reverse.

Throughout my eavesdropping I was particularly taken with the form Mistress Helga's invocation of her Correctness took. She followed the triple resonation of the Mass, perhaps unconsciously, and the Slave too seemed to fall in with this triplicity, responding only when her demand had resounded three times. I could hear come into the Mistress' throat upon the third resounding a kind of catch, as if she quelled some terrible fury, that broke through, anyhow, the restrictive strangulation of her controlled dialectic. It seemed too that the Slave only responded when he heard that catch in her voice, then hurried to submit to its frantic, almost hysterical insistence that she was Correct, and Always Right, and could make blue brown, and black white.

escape from the feminists: a case of true enslavement, charles #106

A tender, ardent nature can be a source of some embarrassment, if not for the gladsome one possessing it, then for its audience, who usually cannot bear to confront the ecstatic level of those passionate effusions. Slave Charles #106 is just such a one, overwrought always by extremes of emotion. Sensitive, sympathetic, and sentimental, in him worshipfulness is first nature. His profession too is one that requires near-martyrdom, a job famous for producing the burnt-out case: he works in a city agency handling cases of child abuse. How, with his all-or-nothing temperament he confronts the daily horrors of his work with intense compassion, keeps his demanding wife and six children happy and content, and maintains the high level of energy needed for the enormous amount of housework we place upon his shoulders is the rare phenomenon of servitude that is Charles #106.

He wishes only to be of service, and draws his strength from his utter selflessness. Whatever whim we may devise he hurries to undertake its realization. A fanatic love for the neat and tidy, his urgency that all cleaning items must be in good repair and of high quality, as well as his fear that We Ourselves might have to somehow sweep, has made him Number One Houseboy in our Theatre. We approve his innovations in method; displeased as he was with his slow progress on his knees about the loft, two sets of hard plastic knee-pads – one for knees, and one for his palms – soon set him literally flying about the perimeter of the Theatre. We cannot prevent ourselves from laughing as he speeds by, wielding the dustrag artfully, perennially sunny smile ashine.

His reward for work well-done is permission to view the Mistress dressed in a leotard, high-heeled boots and boxing gloves. Before he can exclaim in awe he is knocked to the ground, leapt upon and all over pummelled. In finale, his neck might be clamped into a firm scissor-grip. He can remain in perfect peace for hours in various wrestling holds. He is good to practice on as he is a small weakling. I myself prefer the scissor-lock as it leaves my hands free to read or talk on the 'phone.

Charles is poor, lives far from Manhattan, and has to invent elaborate lies to explain his evening stays in the town. As he has to save his lunch-money for two months in order to afford a mere half-hour of our time, we allow him to stay as long as he can. He only annoys at times when he tries to do too many things at once. Dashing about like an overexcited pup that he is, we have more than a few times tripped over him. At such times he can be stowed in a closet, until he calms down enough to carry out one order at a time.

His foot-massages are gentle and exact, his conversation sometimes of a nature to flatter and interest. And always that bright smile that grows even wider when a little pat is tapped upon his balding head.

He has a taste for poetry and will recite his home-made doggerel in our honour, amidst snickers and groans that only increase his pleasure. He has given himself a pen-name too: 3-M, or MMM, which stands for Meagre Male Mind. My personal favourite literary bit of his is the note he left for Mistress Helga, in his usual tiny, childish hand:

> *Dear Mistress Helga,*
> *I just want to thank you for your generosity in*
> *giving me your sandwich crusts.*
> *Thank you sincerely,*
> *MMM*

From time to time he does evidence some angst concerning the lies he must tell his wife when he comes to us. He swears he is extremely submissive at home, but he fears she is at times irked by it. He vouches for her superior intelligence, her more advanced status in her profession, and his willingness to take on all household work. But he is certain he bores and irritates her; excessive compliance can be a bore to one who does not know how to crown themselves with it.

One afternoon we received his usual frantic, stuttering 'phone-call – he was somehow in Manhattan, and with his wife, in a midtown hotel at the annual NOW Convention – Ms. Steinem's original group, the National Organization of Women. He could come right over – his wife was in a seminar, he was supposed to be in another.

We berated him, "You'll forego your feminist education for an afternoon of dusting?"

He claimed the highest honour he could grant feminism was to go where the demands were the greatest.

"There aren't enough powerful women executives there for you? You can't find anyone to worship in a hotel full of feminists?"

They didn't understand – he needed to be low, very low – debase himself before the most Superior, most overweening and whimsical authority.

"You're afraid you're not worthy to be amongst them ..."

"I'm not!" he enthused, "They treat me politely ... I feel like a hypocrite!"

"You can't get anyone to even give you a shove?"

"Oh, why don't they get it ...Why aren't they – more strict?"

Dear little Charles! Not even a thousand modern feminist Women could exhaust the riches he has to offer Womankind.

the chronic, the erratic, and the fantastic

We may posit three categories of client who visit the Dominatrix and her professional Dungeon. First, there are those for whom their specific masochism or submissiveness is the primary reality of their sexuality. Month after month, year after year, their focus does not alter, their needs minusculely change. Their *regular* clients we may call 'chronic'. Only by way of a specialization – a fixed and hardened schemata of perversity – can they achieve sexual satisfaction. (They ought not to be criticized for this – as there are those perverts who never sully convention, never subvert the superego – may we assume that mayhem – not orgasm – rules such psyches?

The second group I term 'erratic', as they come to their Mistress or Master as the sweeping impulse to be punished, indulge in fetish, *et cetera*, comes over them as if from out of 'nowhere'. They of course require the release as exceedingly as does the Chronic, but they differ in that they are very conflicted, ambivalent about their need, would prefer that they did not have the need at all. Such types set up many strict conditions as to the manifestations of this desire, and are very exacting that everything be done just so. This is understandable in that they believe that if they have some ultimate, perfect experience, they will remove the 'sickness' from their being altogether. However, such perfect moments rarely do come, especially with someone in such denial. Even if he has a good catharsis, there is always another day, the desire will return, and the need to alleviate the pressure upon him once more. Even if he returns to the scene of 'perfection', he may be unable to achieve it again. Such is the trial of the erratic, who cannot accept or love his masochism. Such types often become hostile, snide, or rude, reflecting their own self-hatred onto the Mistress, who ought to be greatly honoured as their only means of expressing this faculty.

The third group, the 'fantastic', are those who have lived with a certain idea, or a specific fantasy, concerning their sexuality perhaps for their entire life. They have however refrained from ever acting these ideas out. It may be something as simple as having sex with someone of another race; it may be an idea of torture that no man could ever endure. If they should venture to the Mistress and her Dungeon at last, at best he will have an experience that grants an immediate, earth-shaking catharsis and revelation as to the interior meaning of the ritual they have invented. They are there, kneeling, dressed like a girl; they feel a beating, but once! and they know exactly what it means to them. In possession of this knowledge they quit our precincts, never again (they claim) to need to enter a Theatrical Dungeon. Fantasies may be based on mere technicalities. For example, a client claimed he could not understand why his girlfriend would not submit to anal sex. He could not believe that it hurt that much, and was compassionately inspired to investigate the matter himself. He was of course rendered helpless, and outraged – he admitted his utter stupidity, and begged her forgiveness. We thereupon instructed him in the more loving method.

The 'erratic' are highly interesting in that they are so conflicted. Episodically they require their masochism to flaunt. They generally view the 'session' as a kind of hygienic trial they know they must endure for their sexual and mental health. If they do not 'dispose' of their masochism in this controlled way, they fear more sociopathic forms may leak out into their everyday lives. Or they may already be manifesting sadism in corporate life, or at home, and know they need a curbing.

Even in our exceedingly frank times, with all its glut of information, people remain as stupid as they want to be. The average married woman cannot help viewing an outbreak of male masochism with utter horror. He would instantly lose his mystic quality of manhood, so necessary for love and respect. To allow masculinity to be a crawling, whining dog that begs to be beaten, or worse, is too hard. If asked simply, for example, to slap her husband's face during intercourse in order to promote arousal, a wife may very well burst out crying. The subsequent emotional revulsion he would then receive from her would be essentially destructive to the relationship. Thus it is in the married slave's best interest to circumscribe his masochism, save it up for the Mistress-Master who can suffer him lightly. Masochism can deeply traumatize those who witness it – perhaps not as much as a witnessing of sadism – but it behooves the sufferer to relieve himself of his unsightly burden in the depths of a dungeon of some devising.

It is from the 'chronic' cases that the Superior may have their most rewarding emotional experiences – because we are of course Chronic ourselves. Such clients have achieved a level of self-acceptance and equilibrium concerning their essential perversity. They will never change, they can never be cured, and with a professional they know a stable context, with a person in control of themselves and capable of controlling them. It does happen that salutary transferences occur, and the Mistress can expect affection, deep respect, awe and love from the chronic slave.

Case Of Eddie #9: Chronic Case

Eddie was dominated and controlled by his mother and lived with her until the day she died. When he first came to see me fifteen years ago, he would steal his mother's gigantic corsets and wear them in the session, as he was beaten and tortured. He is fixated upon severe tortures of his very large breasts and genitals. His favoured instrument of torture is a stem of rose thorns. He is only masochist – he manifests no submissiveness but a kind of grudging, "Yeah, okay Mistress." He enjoys some humiliation but is so good-humoured I start laughing as I insist, "You are a rotten, good-for-nothing ... "

He is particularly fond of his rose-bushes, and of course their thorns. The long stems with sharp, bare thorns attached he brings each year at the same time. When I once remarked it was a very bouquet for Morticia Addams ... and perhaps he might one day bring me an *actual bunch of living roses* from his garden, he looked surprised and went into an analysis of the relative sharpness of the thorns, after the roses were dead, versus the thorns of the living bloom. "If you try to dry out the stem from a cut rose, it won't be hard enough. It will bend in your hand and break! We have to wait until the roses die." For what reason would his torturer want a rose whose stem would not be of use?

The day after his mother died Eddie came to the dungeon – and every day thereafter, throughout the entire funeral. We acquired almost a dozen huge, stout corsets in every colour. Throughout the torture session he bitched and complained about his family, his sister, the way the funeral was arranged. He was unable to take his usual measure of pain, and refused to wear the corset. Later on, his pain tolerance came back to its regular level, but he never wore the corsets again. He paid for his several sessions that week from a store of five-dollar bills he had found in his mother's closet. All were brand-new bills, dated 1948, which is the year that Eddie was born.

Case Of David V., Erratic

David V. would arrive in Manhattan and call several times to make certain we had his appointment. He invariably arrived drunk, dishevelled, and late. He is passionately involved with leather, and wants only to stare at a woman dressed thus, who stands over him and looks down on him, muttering imprecations. He kisses and caresses the clothing, almost crying as he does so. He on one occasion insisted that Mistress Angel allow him to buy her a leather outfit. She met him the next day and he spent an inordinate amount on feminine finery, as well as two expensive costumes of leather by a French designer.

Over cocktails, after shopping, David V. assured Mistress Angel he was in great need of someone in his life who would always be there for him, to insult him as he needed. He travels widely, and wanted to be able to telephone at any hour and be told what a bloody fool he was. When she demurred, refusing to give out her personal phone number, he told her that if she would please do this for him, he would write her a check for ten thousand dollars. Of course she humoured him, made certain he had her correct address, but privately considered if he were going to do it, why did he not just write the check that instant?

Two weeks later, an envelope arrived, sloppily addressed and not even sealed. Within floated a real check for the promised amount. Mistress Angel was of course pleased, but she waited in vain for him to call and ask for his 'due'. The check cleared, a month went by, and still not a word from David V. We may shorten this tale by allowing that he did eventually call again, and take his usual session. Upon receiving the gift of her private telephone line, he made use of it less than three times, before disappearing, as the erratic will.

Case Of O.K., One Of The Fantastic

From the wilds of Midwestern America came a letter from Slave O.K., who was answering an ad we ran in *Aggressive Woman* magazine, in which we stated we enjoyed 'fantasies of surgery'. We could consider O.K. a potential murderous psychopath – or merely a lonely soul and eventual suicide. It is odd indeed how death itself never appears within his text, yet no-one could possibly undergo the brutality detailed without surely dying. He has not, in reality, the slightest idea of what such torments would feel like.

"Dearest Mistress:

In the many advertisements one can read in the S&M publications, most sound alike but every once in a while one face, one set of words, one promise of fulfilment of the innermost fantasy is seen, and yours', my dearest Mistress, is that one. Because of my very sensitive position here in B____, it is impossible for me to meet you personally at the moment (even if I were given that unique privilege) but this does not diminish my desires. I have taken the liberty of enclosing a ten page handout which tells of what interests me ... I hope you do not find it offensive or indelicate but touching in you a kindred spirit. I have enclosed a SASE should you care to respond. Until then, Love, O.K."

Thereupon I opened the thick and closely-written manuscript: *The Magnificent Tortures Of The Male.*

"It is nearly impossible to find a Mistress-Torturer who can REALLY DO PENIS AND TESTICLE TORTURE AUTHENTICALLY FOR MOST SAY THEY CAN AND THEN WHAT A DISAPPOINTMENT.

But how hard it is for you, dearest Mistress, to find the perfect male victim, one who really wants knitting needles thrust down his pee hole. Or electrical catheters plunging down his urethral tube, causing him to arch his back, tense his bound arms and legs in a most severe racked spread-eagle position and to scream to the heavens in a sound-proofed dungeon. It is hard to do it I am sure without damaging him permanently!

Is there a man who can take it? Who can take hot, short, razor-sharp pins stuck into the scrotal sac? Vises to clamp the testicles, while she teases him with a vibrator giving him simultaneous pain and pleasure? Is there a woman who really enjoys crushing the scrotal sac in needle-studded gloves, tying a wet leather thong around and around the penile shaft, then sitting and relaxing smoking a cigarette as the man is under an electric heater, drying the thong and causing it to tighten until the sac turns violet? Is there a man who can take pins thrust under the toenails and fingernails, hot and sharp?"

This invocation continued for several pages, as he described more and more brutal torments to the male genitalia, finally winding up with the context in which this will take place:

"The penis-testicle torture-scenarios should include Nazi-Gestapo interrogation of a pilot, Nazi-Gestapo interrogation by Head Nurse who rather than bringing aid and comfort is instructed to get all the information and pain of course is her special way. I think there is nothing more sensually torturing than a black-leather-skirted, Nazi arm-banded woman in high black boots and a starched white

shirt. You have been assigned to get the information for the Highest Authorities, and you love to torture it out of us naive little-boy Americans. In time his body will give out and you will be triumphal once again – proving beyond a doubt that the female is deadlier than the male. In time, the tiny testes, the puny penis, his little tits, his shrivelled mind are in your hands and he screams for you and tells you everything, otherwise you're going to make him come again. In fact, he might tell you more than he really knows.

When there is nothing more to get from him a Sharp, Hot, Jagged knife is then used on him in your final act of victory. By castrating him you have achieved the crowning glory of sensual-erotic superiority.

It is not the brutality that I seek but the exotic excitement of such tortures and the gelding which proves without a doubt that women are superior to men. If only women knew this and stopped being maids, stopped lying on their backs in the missionary position and exerted themselves, dressed the role and clamped their hand on the testicles and squeezed, the world would be a better place in which to live."

[Editor's Note: See Appendix A for the balance of this document]

From these three 'paradigms' of the masochistic/submissive type we might generalise, superficially, that the level of self-acceptance rises towards the Chronic Slave as the most self-loving of the three. Odd, is it not – that the very one who indulges most often, who would be considered thus in the 'normal' world *the most degenerated* – is the one, in my experience, most capable of both giving and receiving the greatest pleasure. In that I mean the Chronic is the healthiest, most psychically integrated, 'friendliest' of slaves, often viewing him or herself with some humour.

It is as well amongst these Chronic ones that the highest possibility for a creative development in sexuality exists. In view of clients known and observed in twenty years of practice, I will hazard to reflect there are two evolutions, which may occur in tandem: the intensity of the masochistic needs abate and/or the sexual orientation of heterosexuality changes into that of homosexuality [see chapter on "Enforced Homosexuality"]. Why this occurs is again a matter for reserved generality. (If nothing else, I have learned that every 'Case' is very different from every other, and I no sooner believe I have pegged a type when the doorbell rings to contradict me.)

The Erratics exist in abundance. Thousands crawl daily from their closets for their thrill, for that brief, shameless moment – happy moment, without shame! – to gaze upon that Ideal Mistress-Master who will 'force' them to their 'worst' – an orgasm. They do not appreciate the irony that all their pleasure is dependant upon rejecting their pitiful fantasy that they are 'Normal'. Their sense of humour is very feeble, and a sense of themselves as doomed, or even diseased, is a prominent feature.

If you, beleaguered reader, have managed to slog through the Fantasist O.K.'s infinite Appendix, and wonder if he ever managed to put down his pen long enough to make the trip to the Dungeon door – the answer is of course: No. Can he really risk finding out that such violence as he purports to desire does not exist except perhaps in the dreams of a serial killer? It seems the more complex and literary the fantasy, the less likely will the fantasist try to enact his designs. This is not to say that O.K. might not have manifested his long madness elsewhere. In a frustrated eruption of self-mutilation... in suicide... or more therapeutically, in writing, writing, writing it all out. He cannot compromise with the understanding Dominatrix, even if her Eye is Hot, Sharp, Jagged... But let us hope at this moment that his great Fantasy is not being fulfilled, in sad milque-toast manner, as a mere projection upon the stern and unsuspecting face of a competent Psychiatric Nurse.

enforced homosexuality

The study of Krafft-Ebing's published cases shows us in masochists the strong homosexual attitude; the withdrawal from a normal sexual partner. Men are impotent; women with pronounced masochistic attitude are anaesthetic at coitus. It is true that the fulfilling of the masochistic fantasy brings with it the orgasm. Yet the analysis of such fantasy shows us again and again that it is precisely the homosexual elements of the fantasy that release the orgasm.[1]

Many men desire to know the pleasures of homosexual sex, and are forced to suppress this desire because of the social stigma that still, in the year 1997, attaches to being overtly homosexual. Compelled by convention to maintain the heterosexual charade, we see how their desire to be with a man is controlled, overshadowed by the Woman they must deal with. If he is fortunate, that Woman may require him to make love to a man. The Woman will 'make him into' a homosexual – by rejecting him for sex; by initiating him into gay-sex; by feminizing him; by 'allowing' him to do whatever he wants with a man. When appropriate, Mistress Angel has encouraged some clients to safely engage in homosexual exchange, but with the plague of AIDS as a taboo upon most, hundreds of men have been thrown back in the Mistress' closet. There the Mistress becomes Master, adept at making from their most complex closetry an agreeable sitting-room, featuring in drapery and cushions what it lacks in windows.

---

[1] Wilhelm Stekel, *Sadism And Masochism.*

Terence Sellers

If he should decide to take the big step and experience sex with a man, it will be with a man that the Mistress has given to him. He may thus exonerate himself from any responsibility in the engagement. He has placed himself under the Woman's control. What happens to him while on 'the other side' is something that has happened *to* him – is most shocking – repellent – exciting. His taboo desire is expressed into the room she has padded for this secret purpose. And, sometimes, magically, without a man actually being present, he becomes as totally homosexual as it is possible for him to be. No-one knows, no-one will ever know, except the Mistress. He may swear allegiance to the phallus, but allows himself to be penetrated only by an artificial toy of a male. Not to be forgotten – all the while it is essential that the Mistress express her displeasure with his behaviour, e.g. discovering that he was all along 'just a faggot'. She cannot be wholly libertine, must remind him of the moral code, which is employed here in transgressive reversal to heighten the pleasure.

We recognize as the important fact of masochism the avoidance of the normal sex act. The psychic impotence of the masochist appears to us no longer to be the consequence of his masochism, but the masochism the result of his psychic impotence. The masochist seeks quite another object than the woman before him, with whom he shows himself to be impotent; the masochism serves to veil his secret sexual goal.[1]

---

[1] Wilhelm Stekel, *Sadism And Masochism*

Dialogue For Fantasy Of Enforced Homosexuality: 'The Faggot Stands Revealed For All To See'

The case of Damen #111, with Mistress Angel Stern and the 'Master Antony'.

It is the 'wedding night' of Angel and Damen. She is sitting in an armchair fully dressed; her naked husband is kneeling before her.

Mistress: It was very disappointing, Damen.

Damen: I know ... I'm so nervous.

Mistress: I think there's something more to it than that.

Damen: No – really – there isn't. I love you. I adore you! Please let me try to please you again.

Mistress: Try? Try? Now I'm to allow you to practice your ineptitude upon me?

Damen: No... no... I guess not. I'm sorry. It must have been disgusting for you.

Mistress: You asked me to marry you under false pretences. I want this marriage annulled – with damages awarded to me.

Damen: No, no – then everyone will know.

Mistress: I want them all to know. I want them all to know – that you are not a man.

Damen: (Grovelling at her feet in desperation) You can't do that... you can't tell the world...

Mistress: That you're gay? Yes I can.

At the word 'gay' Damen begins to react as though he were having convulsions. As well his excitement is intensely apparent.

Damen: (Close to weeping) How can you say that to me... how can you say that...

Mistress: That you're gay? That you might even be... a cocksucker?

Damen: Oh, God, no – not that! (Wailing)

Mistress: I'm calling my friends – I have to tell them – this is just too traumatic for me. I'm calling my best friend – he has to know...

Damen: He? Who is... he?

Mistress: The Master Antony. He's an expert on cocksucking.
Damen: Stop saying that... stop saying that word.
(Convulsing)
Mistress: (Pretending to be on the phone) Hello, Antony?
This is Angel, and this is the wedding night! What a joke! I know
you warned me about Damen, but I didn't believe you! Darling –
you were right – it's true. He couldn't do the deed, and now he's
lying at my feet with an enormous erection, *at last*, when I told him
I thought he might be a *faggot*!
Damen: Please don't divorce me... let me live with you...
and Master Antony.
Mistress: Now he's saying he'll gladly serve us both, if only
I won't tell the world that he's a *queer*!
Damen: You can even have sex with other men, anyone
you want. I'll go out and find men for you...
Mistress: You'll go cruising for me? But won't you just bring
home a sissy panty-waist like yourself, someone you can make
brownies with, someone you can be sisters with? What do you
know about manhood, anyway?
Damen: I know what a real man is. I know. I know – it's
not me.

*The sound of heavy male footsteps are heard in the next room.
Damen looks disturbed, cowers from the sound.*

Mistress: Oh, it must be Master Antony, here in your
mother's house. I told him how to get into the house – I told him
which bedroom we were in – the Master bedroom, that your mother
let us sleep in tonight. Where you're supposed to be fucking your
new bride. Here, in your mother's bedroom – you're going to be the
bride, Damen. We'll find out who the Master is tonight.
Damen: It's not me.
Mistress: No, baby, it's not you. Now let's dress you – let's
get you ready for your defloration.
Damen: I'm going to lose my cherry.
Mistress: You're just a little girl, an innocent thing – oh I
hope The Master will not be too cruel to you.

Damen is dressed in women's fancy-dress, all in white, with excessive ruffles and restrictive, rubberized underwear such as fat women favour.

Mistress: Now you're very beautiful. I'm leaving you alone, in the bridal chamber. Your husband is coming, darling. Open up your body and soul to him – let him take you where *all women* go.
Damen: Don't leave me! Don't leave me alone with him! What if I don't please him?
Mistress: Then you'll be thrown out onto the garbage-heap of the world as useless to both women and men. You'll be ground into meat for dogs.
Damen: Then I must please him.
Mistress: You have to. You have no choice. You have no choice – because you want to. This is the day you've been waiting for your entire life. When at last you'll get your lips around a man. You'll be having sex for hours and hours, with a man, the Master Antony, a real man. You'll have to give up to his every dirty pleasure. You'll open your body to his violent ravagement. You'll drink his come, drink his piss...
Damen: Yes – yes! I'll do everything!
Mistress: That's right, pussy, say yes, little queer! You'll have to say Yes to his every command.
Damen: Oh, is that him? (Staring at the door)

Sound of heavy footsteps without; door to the room opens slightly. Damen experiences his ultimate pleasure.

Here Damen #111 becomes a woman who is frail, nervous and virginal. 'The woman before him' rejects him, 'forces' him to admit he desires a homosexual love. As she devalues him as a sex-object for herself, she gives him thereby his true value – he is affirmed as 'gay'. She then prepares him for his 'proper' marriage to an Ideal Male. The imminent presence of this potent Virility (whose heavy step is simulated by a lady in riding boots) brings him to ecstasy. The homosexual man – the one he truly worships and desperately needs – is the lover he will in the flesh never allow himself to know. This would be rather tragic if the masochism were not there to extract bliss from his acute, but preferred, frustration.

cryptohomosexuality: case of john #21

When John first applied to Mistress Angel Stern in 1985 at the age of thirty for a bondage, verbal humiliation, caning and whipping, he stated that he had never submitted to such treatment before. Still, he did not want the Mistress to be gentle with him – he requested that she be as severe as she was able, especially in the use of the 'dog whip' – twelve inches long, thing and lithe and prone to cutting. The Mistress was accustomed to new slaves requesting her worst – only to discern that they possessed no pain tolerance at all.

There was at first no response to her standard verbal repartee. He knelt before her as she commanded him, "Confess."

But he could say nothing – not unusual in the novice who has yet to discover the freedom there is in taking on a role.

"You know you deserve to be punished." Still no answer. "We can see by the way you hold your head – the hunch of your shoulders – that you can't meet my eye – that you are guilty." Silence. "It doesn't matter what you've done. Even if you've done nothing – you're planning something. You know I am a great believer in preventative discipline. Suffer now, to avoid future crimes."

John's mouth opened at last, "Yes Mistress – punish me. Punish me severely – for having ... thought ... for having homosexual thoughts!" And so the thematic emerged.

"Indeed? Only thoughts? You have not indulged your body – you have not pleasured yourself?"

"No, Mistress."

"You don't sound sure. You have definitely – NEVER –

masturbated to these thoughts?

"No, Mistress."

"I believe that is a lie. You are to be punished for the thoughts, and for lying as well."

John was directed to the bondage-table, where he lay down in full submission to 'the worst'.

John was tied down to the ordinary refrain: *Your body is out of control. You have lost control of your body. Now it belongs to me – it is my body – and I will do with it what I will.* Once firmly affixed to the table, the punishment began: light strokes of the cane, rhythmic and sure. Noting with interest the irritated 'tsks' and sighs emanating from his agitated form, she began to lay on much harder strokes, until his breathing grew more regularly passionate. For it was evident he possessed a naturally high tolerance for pain, a state sometimes unknown to the novice himself.

Now would chime in the litany of abuse: *naughty sissy, baby-boy, not-really-a-boy-but-a-pussy, little faggot, secret cocksucking toy, queer-bait, boy-hole, powder-puff.* Throughout his face remained serious and remote.

"How rebellious! Showing me how hard you can be, are you? It seems you are – unrepentant! You're not insulted when I call you – FAG!"

The situation demanded that some response from him be forthcoming, as the punishment was verging towards the breaking of skin and blood.

"You think you can take the worst, don't you? You're going to be sorry you challenged me. Are we going to make you scream, boy?"

Now the Mistress sensed the air charge up as he registered her threats.

The Mistress set then to beating him with her full strength – stopping only to stroke and quiet the whip, to soothe it in its travails. And still John needed more – she could smell it – he was out of his body, not present, riding the pain towards some private nirvana. Blow after blow went down, she pressing on through near exhaustion. Now the insinuating pleasure of her own self evanescing came upon her as she gazed down at her handiwork: the bound and wretched body crossed over with darkening weals. All at once a demonic fury possessed her – a thing not from herself, but as in transmission come from the ruin of his body, as she hooked onto the traumatic charge that now flowed freely with the blood. As the physical body is particularly wounded, so the subtle 'astral' body, in trauma prior-wounded, impresses on the Operator its First Bleeding – and, in the Mistress, eliciting no compassion but her own deep psychic sadism. Thus was she seized with a true disgust for the feeble, white, feminine frailty of the 'boy' before her, lashed out at him wildly – so he screamed. And when she heard that scream she could not help but laugh. Real terror in that shriek of his! Like a child's cry, so awful it calls up no civilised reaction but a deeper streak of triumph, revelling like a beast in the conquering, perfect control she held over that helpless boy-in-man for an ecstatic instant.

... the man had jerked and the whip had gone astray, curled round his inner thigh and snipped at a testicle. As he writhed in agony, screamed and burst into tears, he heard her laugh – he heard that short, triumphant laugh ... he groaned aloud as he felt his half-limp penis ejaculate.

"Oh how did you know – how did you know?"

As the Mistress began to untie him, she shortly apologised – for after all she had not meant to strike him on that dangerous spot. The contrast of her courtesy with the unmitigated cruelty curled him into a foetal position, whereupon he began to sob without restraint. She sat by him and allowed him to cling to her, stroking him kindly to soften the release of what she thought was only severe physical pain. As she quietly spoke to him, she began to draw forth a pathetic etiology the pain had elicited.

It was not true that he had never submitted to such treatment before. An utterly helpless physical state ... accusations of a 'loathsome' sexuality ... the caning and especially *the curling round of the tip of the whip* had all taken place before. He had experienced it all before – at the hands of his father.

As a boy, both he and his younger brother had been forced to regularly submit to this sadistic form of punishing children. The father was quite adamant on the subject of their manhood – he beat them to make them strong – to make them men – he beat them to make them hard. Were they men, or were they faggots? Only sissies cried. Still shuddering, John exclaimed that my 'accident', emerging spontaneously from my mediumistic fury, had been the very pain that had always broken him.

"And Father would laugh, too – he would laugh as I screamed – just as you did."

He tried to get hold of himself to leave, apologising for his hysteria. The Mistress assured him she didn't mind if he cried. The tears continued to flow, and flow as he then confessed to suffering along yet another strata of torment. His younger brother, with whom he had in tandem been punished, had only recently died of AIDS. He described his brother lovingly as having been very beautiful – "Not like me!" – who had, from an early age, in wild defiance of Father, been not only flagrantly gay but wildly promiscuous – and, right from the start of his homosexual life had too favoured erotic punishment.

"I'll never forget the first time he showed me the whip-marks all over his body. He had let himself be whipped in public by strange men. Then he had given himself over to be raped by just anyone ... in the backroom of some horrible place."

His brother had bragged about how much pain he could take – that he could take *anything* that random brutality had to offer.

When asked what the father's reaction had been to his son's illness, John replied, "That's the amazing thing – for the first time in our lives, our father was there. He did everything he could for my brother – took care of him, with his own hands."

As per Ducasse: the torturer's hands lovingly return to the scene of the crime to bathe the wounds *he had himself inflicted.*

"He came to the hospital every day ... and, when my brother died, my father and I held each other, and cried."

John curled more vehemently into the foetal position, "I couldn't remember the last time my father had held me." He shuddered, "I can't help it. I still hate him."

The Mistress gently suggested that while his father was still open and vulnerable that John might bring up the topic of his abuse.

"Oh, HE knows!" came the harsh cry, "He blames himself – he knows all about the gay life-style, the kinky sex. He knows what he did to my brother. For the first time in my life – I've seen my father suffer!"

"Very well," replied the Mistress, "but what about the *other person* who was still suffering? What of the present person still standing before him. Don't you want to hear your father say to you too – 'I'm sorry for what I did'?"

John seemed to collapse, "I can't do that to him ... it would be the last straw – it would kill him."

The relentless Mistress went on, "But don't you want him to die?"

Like his brother before him, John loves the man who makes him suffer most shamefully. The father's own fearsome homosexual interest in his sons was the probable cause of his attacks upon them. *The father corrupted the innocence of his sons as he punished them to guarantee it.* He invoked for them a lover who was not yet there, awakened in his boys a fantasy of an unspeakably sexual male. While his brother rushed to embrace that forbidden, John was and is trapped in a strange limbo of feeling desire for a man who is not there. Before this phantom, and the remote father, and now the brother who is dead – before all these absences who he has been made ashamed to embrace, he poignantly weeps.

His masochism further impels him to martyr himself to his father. When given by Fate a rational opportunity to relieve some of his anguish, to at last accuse his father and perhaps forgive him – he refuses. For he loves the man so much he would not seek to punish him for his real crimes. For the moment, the brother has well-accomplished the punishment of Father – taken up with his own hand the wretched prophecy – indeed become one of the reviled 'dirty queers'. But in John has the taboo against being 'gay' been *fully obeyed.* He will *not* be with a man – no he *is* with a woman – but a woman as 'bad' as he is – a pervert, 'whore', and sadomasochist. With this 'bad woman', as with the bad father, he may have the pleasure allotted his kind: the pleasure of being homosexual, and punished for it. With a woman he at least need not suffer the superadded torment of adoring his tormentor, might abandon himself too to an orgasm he would have to hide from beloved, angry Dad.

John assured Mistress Angel that he had never sought homosexual contact – nor would he ever. Yet neither had he yet had a 'normal' heterosexual affair. At the age of thirty, having come of age in an era of the freest possible morals, John was still a virgin.

"She has to be a special woman. She has to understand me. But how can I tell a nice woman, someone good enough to marry, that I might need – this?" and he indicated the gloomy dungeon-room. "I've got to get it out of my system – you can help me – help me purge myself. I want to be normal!"

John still believes in his father's formula: revile the body, drive out the demon Queer/demon Masochist; be cleansed of all impurity and be made holy enough for some mythic Pure Woman. This he will achieve through a purgatorial congress with a kind of Witch. To him this makes sense – as he is yet unholy, he deserves only the company of devils. John does not understand that the die is cast – his corruption is innate – this Hell is his home.

Passing through dozens of trials of exorcism, John discovers he is not becoming any cleaner, holier, or any less obsessed with incipient Queerness. The pain returns ... the beatings go on ... when one demoness does not effect the magic change, he seeks out another. He earns a slave number we see him so frequently. Some five years pass and he is seen to become the 'personal slave' of the lovely Mistress Brenda.

John takes his Mistress Brenda shopping, makes dinner for her at her apartment, is permitted to play valet and is sometimes allowed to call her on the 'phone when he is depressed. An exception to the rule against personal involvement has been made for him, in part due to his tragic history, but also as he is of a character mild, well-bred and self-effacing. His need to be tied down, whipped, 'snipped' and psychologically ravaged has not abated much, but he interrupts the session often before it comes to the crisis. Mistress

Terence Sellers

Brenda of course allows no sexual intimacy, nor has she cultivated any aspect of his homosexuality, as Mistress Angel might have ventured. He is kept 'encrypted', neurotic and stunted, and requires only a certain bit of mothering attention. The main, ostensible cause of his depression is the fate of his brother, but neither has he yet confronted his father with the crimes against himself, poor John.

We prefer the term 'crypto-' and 'encrypted' over the modern 'closeted' in describing this form of homosexuality as the prognosis for John ever becoming healthily manifest so is nil. He determines that it shall remain buried, and its expressions, as we observe in the dungeon, are a cryptoglyph for all that is shameful, painful, erotic and deadly. In such a case, considerations other than that of sexual health, or personal sexual satisfaction are at stake. Obedience to authority, heterosexuality, and the Ideal of purity buries true pleasure beneath their conventional weight. While men often seek out women or men in the professional sexual field to enjoy a forbidden form of sex, in the case of John #21, we see he does not use the professional to indulge himself, but as the only way for him to have any relationship at all. He is not hypocritical enough (yet) to think himself 'straight', marry a woman, and expect her to tolerate his probable impotence. Mistress Brenda knows his whole life story, socializes with him, makes no sexual demands and provides companionship. This 'Victorian marriage' may be the greatest happiness John will ever know.

Postscript On The Case Of John #21

By 1994 Mistress Pamela Cameron, a young Mistress with a background in psychology and physical therapy, had been administering to John and granted us a development report on his evolved particularities. As far as she was concerned his taste for punishment continued to be extreme. His sessions, extending beyond two hours at a time, manifested a near-unconquerable tolerance for the cane and whip. Extremes of torment visited upon his genitals as well left him unflapped. Mistress Cameron could assert that she found John #21 a most gratifying subject, as her sadism need observe no bounds but that of a rational thought, now and then, for his safety, as the flow of blood was viewed by him as a commonplace matter of indifference.

A new wrinkle had unfolded in the life of John, it seemed. He arrives with a shopping bag full of brand-new ladies' garments: everything from underwear to shoes, always the new dress, a wig and set of make-up. Prior to all torment John insists on being disguised as a female: then overpowered, stripped and violated as per usual. How this pretext to his usual ordeal evolved necessarily we may speculate: it is more than the typical psychic diversionary tactic of the transvestite, so that it is 'not John' abducted, humiliated, bound and hurt but a schizoid invention. (She/he cries out in a high-pitched voice for 'help', but otherwise does not manifest the higher refinement in manners of most transvestites.) That his feminine wardrobe is always new, costly, and at times based on 'themes' – e.g. at Xmastime an entire red-lace negligée ensemble – proves that he continues to pursue his Ideal – he would know and be sexual as a neat, clean, 'beautiful' Good-woman who undeservedly, but naturally must suffer at the hands of the Mad Bad and Dangerous-To-Know Dominatrix who rules over his real sex-life.

Mistress Cameron surprised us in claiming that John #21 has never expressed to her any ambivalence concerning his perversity. Never has she heard a plea for a 'cure'; indeed he is greatly involved in the minutiae of his sessions, planning and going over the logistics for the next. We may assume in the course of these nine years that he has concluded that a relatively safe and well-controlled expression of the tenets of his sexual education must for now be his greatest pleasure. As long as some sexuality is permitted voice, we expect him to evolve – though in what direction no-one can predict. Mistress Angel was pleased to know that he had thrown off that conventional pressure for 'cure', though the calls his sad frustration make upon him still are far from deep health. His sexuality remains an obedience to his dear beloved – dear Father – and He no-one else can yet compete with.

the catholic religion as a sadomasochistic cult

The religion of love of one's neighbour came to grief upon the splitting of love into its two components – spiritual, and physical – the first of which became virtue, and the second, sin. It led men to deny themselves and to suffer; it gave them pleasure in suffering. Those who suffer become cruel.[1]

The formula to prepare a demonology: Become Sexual.

The immutable condition of being flesh is to know Evil, to sin through flesh. Avoid all occasion of this sin – ignore the body's rampant imperatives! So whilst in Hell captive we *must* deny this Hell. But it cannot be denied – for we burn and are burning up with every desire – what pleasure! Fear! and know disgust, and as you crush your sex, we assure you a high place in our holy hierarchy.

Martyr these base instincts to the unknown Will of our God – pleasure, for its own sake, must be destroyed! (But it cannot be destroyed – it only comes to be tainted through and through with guilt.)

In the young and vulnerable mind – upon which the Catholic religion impresses the full weight of its proscriptions – the tainting of sex with guilt may induce the masochistic appreciation of sex. Observers of the sexually-abused know that once a control is gained

---

[1] Wilhelm Stekel, *Sadism And Masochism.*

Terence Sellers

over a child's sex, the controller in a sense has a victim for life. Any number of perversities may be transmitted, and no-one in our past, present and future society has ever been able to fully control it.

The efforts of the tormented one to throw off the curse of this interference will always be more or less informed by the elements of the early, sometimes unsavoury, control. This applies to the influence of both rude perverts, and the meddling Christians who would also horrify us. Yet even if trampled down, desire *will* be expressed. Sexuality must at first manifest through the fear, disgust and self-hatred the abuse has afflicted them with. Yet through sex's alchemical panacea, these nauseas may be translated into forms of pleasure. We emphasize these forms may be transitional, and so never to be too rigidly suppressed. Desire *must* be expressed, even in its trampled forms. The sexually-abused typically find pleasure in abusing. There should be nothing wrong in behaving thus sadistically, as long as one's partners have given full consent to the pain.[1] Nor, if involutedly masochistic, we will have a taste to suffer on our Cross, know the torments, die, and be buried.

Nuns and priests, devout parents enforce upon children rigours of self-denial only a hardened ascetic or deadened prude might attain to. Do they enjoy their trimming, pruning, hacking away – their castrations? Certainly they have *not* assured themselves of their victims' full consent. But, of course, it's for the good of our souls.

In order to survive this interference, we learned to *appear* to obey – all rules were abided by. We hid whatever pleasures we discovered, for if we did not, and our happiness was observed by our Overseers, we had to support their anger – their at times almost *ecstatic* displeasure with us. And there was never a punishment without an attendant unbearable humiliation – often performed in public. You would long for the physical attack, just so they might stop saying those terrible things to you, phrases like curses upon your life: *your growth will be stunted ... you'll go to Hell ... your*

---

[1] This assumes on everyone's part a level of sophistication only found in a tiny and well-educated sector of the public. No child, either, can give *full* consent.

brain will soften, you will go blind ... God cannot love you if you do that. But once you understood you were anyway doomed for Hell, you merely became adept in ferreting out any brief instant of that sublime ecstatic charge you knew how to find, one layer of clothing away, behind a door with a lock still upon it. And as one became more private, and gained in self-knowledge, and knew others to be acting as one did, with fear and detestation did we perceive the evil control that had been wielded against our sex. No respect for such a religion could survive, only the desire to further escape. For good Catholics – the true slaves – accept this harnessing for life.

How do the torments of a proper repression become at all acceptable to the sincere Catholic? Through the miracle of the Sacrifice ... we offer up our trampled genitalia, we offer them up to God, as a sacrifice for His Glory. We burn up our burning, wash ourselves clean, turn our backs on ever-flourishing evil ... and my God the miracle does occur! The suffering *changes* in quality, loses its sharpness, becomes as a languor ... leaving the mere genitalia to explore the entire body. It is mystic ecstasy ... and as we continue to pray this warm terror spreads and flows through us as before our inner eye we see the beauteous face of Mary, Jesus is in us, God is upon us, we are no longer empty! Blessed be the castrate, as he might come against the very punishing hand of God!

Those who restrain desire, do so because theirs is weak enough to be restrained; and the restrainer or reason usurps its place and governs the unwilling.
And being restrained, it by degrees becomes passive, till it is only the shadow of desire.[1]

Desire bound in a chastity-belt, even desire in a castrate does not *totally* go away. It only takes another form, perhaps exalted, sublime, 'offered up' – or, in sex-crime, a form not so sublime. It is unfortunate our erstwhile *controllers* are not *clearer* about exactly *where* our incorrect, excessive, rampant, horrifying sexuality *ought*

---

[1] William Blake, The Voice Of The Devil, in *The Marriage Of Heaven And Hell.*

Terence Sellers

to go. This is their crude ignorance, and this their failure – without any direction but a 'no' they are the real cause of sexual crime.

Offer it up? Where? To what? We who are unable to conform to the holy constraints are now advised that we have no choice to make the *ultimate* sacrifice. (Ah, may we savour yet more abuse from these pure ones!) We shall abstain from sex *altogether*, upon the pain of eternal damnation, lest we destroy our immortal soul. Could it be possible for a God to deeply hate us so?

Or – could it be – that your holy servants may have failed to really understand You Lord? They thought they grasped the whole of you – bring them to their knees, make them humble again! Puffed up with pride, they have failed in perfect submission, my God! But only you may punish us, Lord – and what this punishment might be – if it might be – can even they foresee and pre-inflict? They have taken your scourge into their own hands, used it for their private pleasures – made this world a hell for us!

If we should act upon our loves and lusts in the manner suggested by our body's happiest instinct – for it is an instrument of Nature, wiser far than usurping Reason! – is this not better? Or, we must admit that it were better for the Soul of Mankind if certain strange realities *never came* into the light – *were never spoken of, never seen.* They would thereby *assuredly* never be done! Thus we who have the Knowledge take on every burden of the 'unnatural', and must accept our incarcerations. Would it not be more of a mercy then if we might also die – and quickly? Yet to commit suicide is also their crime – oh radiant double-bind of torment! They would have us live, to torment us more exquisitely!

Let us imagine that we are willing forever to elide our 'criminal' sexuality. So that we may be yet further assured of the holiness behind this abstention, we are welcomed into the rank of the Elect, where the collar and the veil attaches to the happy celibate. Thus, from the cream of their victim-crop, do they recruit for the holy Office of Repressor – forever and ever, amen. Crypto-homosexuals, furtive caressers of boys; terrified perverts, running in desperation to a God who in time will become as intolerable as their weird desire; certain species of sadistic female, control-freaks, bitter rejects from the courses of love; and other neurotic substrata unfit for human embrace but pure enough for induction into the Lord's company. Amongst them we might find the world's firmest believers in the powers of Satan, and no wonder – for his visitations are surely the only time they are permitted a stroke of pleasure.

In our case that follows, of Jed #17, attempts to twist away from the strictures of his Catholic youth are demonstrated in the wildest need for debasement: for orgasm to occur, his sex must be unbearably humiliated. As a former seminarian, Jed is most poignantly still in thrall. In his tortured genuflexions to the 'Satan', we clearly see that pleasure may only be realized when strained through the imagery of the inhibitive religion.

fantasy of satan: case of jed #17

Jed is on the petite side, handsome, wiry, in his late twenties. Fantasy of Satanic possession: Satan enters his body and makes him do sexual things against his will. Claims to have spent his teenage years in a seminary, before failing to take the Holy Orders. Costuming during the session consists of a priest's starched white collar and nothing else.

In his fantasy he is the Head of a local boys' school called St. Ann's. He is disturbed, because now living in the house next door is a Brazen Harlot, flaunting herself shamelessly before the impressionable eyes of his boys. Her lewd vapours are spreading into the sanctified dormitories, where tragic evidence of an unbridled sexuality is growing amongst the boys. Her depraved rock and roll music can be heard in the classrooms, and when she walks out of her house, dressed provocatively, discipline goes to pieces. Already there is a rumour she has led a boy astray, waylaying him with an invitation to fornication.

Father Jed has sent for the Harlot, so she may be admonished for her seductiveness, demoralizing as it is to Christian youth. She enters his office dressed in tight leather from head to foot, and high-heeled shoes. She strolls around the office, ignoring his request that she be seated, lights a cigarette and throws the match on the floor.

Priest: Madame! You know why I have requested your presence.
Harlot: No, why, babe?
Priest: It has come to our attention that you have entertained a boy of St. Ann's... in what might be called an *objectionable* manner.
Harlot: Mmmm... never had a complaint yet.

Priest: Your behaviour is not... *seemly.*

Harlot: Huh?

Priest: I must request that you stop attempting to practice your depravity upon these innocents.

Harlot: I don't know what you're talking about. I don't need any practice!

Priest: You know what I mean. Cease at once from your influence!

Harlot: I think they're all kind of enjoying my influence.

Priest: I don't care if they're enjoying it, or not. That's nothing for you to concern yourself with, but it is mine. I am in charge of their education!

Harlot: I guess I am too.

She says this as she is come very close to him and looking into his eyes.

Priest: You are... you are worse than I ever imagined.

Harlot: Mmm, aren't I though?

Priest: Oh God – I need your help and protection now! I see now what those poor boys are suffering.

Harlot: Do you? Do you see me? Are you really seeing me?

Priest: I see... I see Satan!

At the magic word he slides to the floor and begins the convulsions of a beached fish.

Priest: I'm falling, I'm falling, Lord, under the influence of this demon. Save me, Jesus!

Harlot: That's where I like to see men – lying at my feet and squirming away like the worms they are!

Priest: God how she laughs, she laughs! She is so evil! She is the worm, Lord, the great Worm of Satan!

Harlot gives him a vicious kick to the crotch, which only exacerbates his frenzy.

Harlot: So we're both worms – so what else is new? But if I'm a worm, why are you the one crawling under my heel?

Priest: I'm not at your heel... I'm at the foot of God. I'm praying,

I'm praying at the foot of God.

Harlot: That's Goddess, fool, and it looks more like you're masturbating.

Priest: Blasphemy! Filth and blasphemy, before a servant of God!

Harlot brings her foot close to the face of the Priest, in threat. He grips it in both hands and inhales of its scent.

Priest: Jesus help me, help me, Satan is making me kiss his hoof. I cannot do it, I cannot...

He is shaking all over, trying to push the foot away at the same time that he raises his face towards it.

Priest: Take this cup from me Lord, take this bitter cup from me, don't make me! Aah!

Harlot: (Wrenches her foot away) That hurts! You're insane, you know that? You're not fit to care for children!

Priest: (Staring at her foot) Hoof of satan.

Harlot: (Kicking him again) Bugger off! I'm getting out of here. You're just blaming Satan for what you want to do.

Priest: You thrust your foot shamelessly before the face of a weak man, and then laugh at his fall.

Harlot: You don't know a thing about kissing feet, or probably anything else to do with sex. You're going to have to be thoroughly trained in how to please a woman.

Priest: No, No, NO!! (Screaming)

Harlot: Christ! Is there a drink in this place? I just know a priest has got to have a stash of liquor somewhere.

Priest crawls slowly to a cabinet and opens it, revealing a row of bottles.

Harlot: See how eager the servant of God is to serve me.

Priest: Satan has me in his hand... I'm doomed. (Fixes a drink)

Harlot: Well, if I can't make you into a decent sex-slave, which might be the case... you're a little worn-out, frayed around the edges... you might make a good valet.

Priest: Madame. I will always be a man of the cloth.

Harlot: I've heard they make excellent valets. Particularly when they've been defrocked.

Priest: (Groaning aloud) Oh Jesus strike me dead, strike me dead now, before I am forced into the slavery of the Arch-Fiend!

Harlot: (Holding him down with her foot) We have you now. Too late.

Priest: Is this what you do to my boys?

Harlot: At first. Then I strip them naked and make them my pets.

Priest: How many... how many have you corrupted?

Harlot: I'm going to have all of them in my power – along with you.

Father Jed is now reaching the final paroxysm, and flings his body back and forth across the floor like a hooked trout.

Priest: I'm ACCURSED... Satan is in my body, Satan's inside me, he's in my body...

Harlot: You're my servant.

Priest: I am your servant, divine Sataness.

Jed often returns after his first hour to continue his fantasy; hence the Mistress should give him some pretext upon which to return. In this case, the Mistress ordered him to "bring one of his boys with him, that night", to her house.

The Priest is knocking upon the Harlot's door.

Harlot: Where is my boy of the evening?

Priest: Madame... please don't ask that of me.

Harlot: You're a liar, and a bad valet. You will have to be punished, severely, beyond your capacity.

Priest: Madame! This time I must stick to the point... the fact remains that a scandal is growing in the community, and I have been charged with... with your repentance.

Harlot: Ha, ha, ha!

Priest: These boys are minors! It is illegal, as well as immoral, to tamper with their innocence! If you continue to ignore these warnings, we will be forced to go to the District Attorney.

Harlot: Oh, him. He's into bondage and suspension.

Priest: You must listen to reason. I want to help you. I pity you.
Harlot: Can it... Go back to the school and bring me little Artie.
Priest: You must keep your hands off them.
Harlot: Jealous, hmm? You want them all to yourself.
Priest: What are you talking about... more and more vileness, a never-ending stream of filth and nightmare from your lips.

Harlot attacks him, throwing him down on the couch and straddling him, lights a cigarette and blows smoke in his face.

Harlot: I think we'd better have a serious discussion here about those boys of yours.
Priest: There is nothing to discuss, Satan...
Harlot: Stop wriggling... you're going to admit to me now, that *you* are the one having constant *unclean* thoughts about those boys.
Priest: Unhand me Satan... it's you, it's you having those ideas.
Harlot: Mmm, reading my mind, are we? Well then I can read yours, and I say it's you having the thoughts, of touching them, adoring them... you're queer for them!
Priest: NO! It's you!
Harlot: Yes, I admit it's me, but it's you, too. We're partners in crime!
Priest: No, no, NO!!!

As he lets loose the paroxysmal scream, she wrestles him down and twists his arms behind his back.

Harlot: You have thoughts... you have those thoughts. The boys have told me... the boys have told me... the boys have told me things about you. They can *smell* you.
Priest: You have obviously corrupted them into having unclean fantasies... None of it is true.
Harlot: You go into the shower-room. You stand around in the shower-room, and look.
Priest: Sometimes the poor things... are seduced into oral copulation. I have to make sure...
Harlot: Sure of what? Make sure of what, of who is the most beautiful, who has the prettiest...
Priest: DON'T SAY IT! Lord, Lord, make Satan stop these evil

words, make her stop!

Harlot: Don't lie in the face of God! Tell the truth! Tell me... tell me how you are UNCLEAN!

He slides out from beneath her onto the floor and commences the convulsive movements of 'possession', as he is forced to confess.

Priest: Father forgive me for I have sinned. I have on more than one occasion had unclean thoughts about those innocent children. I do here confess...

Harlot: I thought so! And what else?

Priest: I have on some... three occasions... had unclean physical contact with one child, from his innocent body derived... an uncleanly... uncleanly...

Harlot: You came?

Priest: No, NO! It was Satan, Satan took me over, it wasn't my fault, it wasn't, oh God forgive me my unholy weakness.

Harlot: We'll have you defrocked. Then you can come live with me and wear *my* frocks!

Priest: I want God to tear it off me... tear this thing off me, destroy this tool of Satan!

Priest writhes at her feet, flexing and jack-knifing as though in terrible pain. He grips his penis and screams.

Harlot: Tool of Satan? I don't think so. His is a lot bigger...

Priest: Bitch! WHORE! I'll cut out your vagina!

Note to Mistresses: When he starts in on the female mutilation (he doesn't always) use the crop and hit him with all your strength. Very high pain tolerance at this point.

Priest: Take me to your castle, Satan, take me to your castle, hide me from the eyes of God!

Harlot: Dummy. You should know by now God sees everything.

Priest: He sees me... he sees me now. God, please forgive me.

Harlot: No.

Terence Sellers

We may derive from this cathartic drama the following probabilities: a seduction of Jed, while a seminarian, by a priest who may have expressed remorse before, during or after sex in terms of a Satanic infusion. This did not make the sex less sexy – the cries of remorse only became incorporated into the sexuality expressed. As well, there may have followed seductions by Jed, of boys younger and inexperienced, for which he still feels pangs of guilt admixed with excitement. I would even venture to say Jed could be at present a priest – horribly conflicted about a homosexuality still imperfectly repressed, for which he cannot, on his own, punish himself severely enough. Thus he enjoins another to punish him for it. The naked priest, whose collar is as a halo above the erect member, is a hallucinated figure from this past, titillating in its wrongness, horrifying in its pleasingness.

The role of the Dominatrix is that of ringmaster of desire – she is the pretext for the outpouring of lust that the celibate, holy, homosexual 'good man' would stop. Elicit desire, to punish desire: the Puritanical codex. There very possibly was never any form of 'harlot' active in the past scenes: she is a projection of Jed's own wanton, unacceptable sexuality. She cannot be contained, she will *not* be punished, she is blasé, sarcastic, knows all, sees all... and laughs. She observes honestly how sex lives in every soul, "and don't blame Satan for it." Satan 'in his body' we may translate as the 'unholy' coital intromission.

As both seducee and seducer, Jed is in agony, and can only be forgiven by invoking a figure of the most loathsome Evil possible: the Harlot, servant of satan. She ought to have her vagina cut out! But is She not also himself, the rampant 'female', passive homosexual boy he harbours – who would love to destroy his own 'vagina'? Hence both his own, and the Mistress' need to impose the most severe punishment at these outbursts of self-loathing. He seems to barely feel the blows, as they drive him over the brink, into cathexis. Satan wins. Through orgasm he has sinned, and died: the priest is dead, and all is calm again.

The apparent foot-fetishism is another blinder, employed to further humiliate his sex and drive him from the 'normal'. He derives no

real pleasure in the foot, is not sensual with it as is the true fetishist. The same follows in the leather-fetish: he is not interested in that skin, only seeks it as it firmly encloses and hides away the undesired female form. Thus, with all preventatives intact, the Mistress may force out of him the true desire: homosexual, here involved with pederasty as well. The holy man is exposed as a hypocrite,
and unholy desire expelled, expressed 'cleanly', with no innocent person being a witness thereof.

The resonant "No" at the end, that refusal to forgive, is not some Furyism, that his crime is so great. No! It is the Nihilist affirmation! There shall be no forgiveness, as there was no crime! We sadomasochists thwart that punishing religion by admitting to the wild sexual pleasure to be had in their punishments. We accept and love these restraints, as a spur to yet greater pleasures! We too insist upon strict prohibitions, in regard to sex-function – we however reserve the right to determine, invent and impose our own interesting by-laws.

If we understand that Right and Wrong is an Ideal invented, while Good and Evil too floats above, in vague and constant gyration... one twists and turns this way and that, to find where one might stand wholly in the Light... so we will prefer at last to dispense with both tiresome Christians and Satanists. Unless of course, we are in the mood to whip up a little torture.

Terence Sellers

fantasy of a satanic cult: from the desk of candy bishop, queen witch for the 'souls of satan' coven

Dear Mistress:

I am answering your ad in *Aggressive Woman* magazine because I am looking for a woman who like a bird of prey can sink her talons in and never let go. My father recently died and I have come into an inheritance, so I don't have to work like I used to, and I'm looking for someone to take over a good, rich slave I've got and keep on him and take him like I used to.

My name is Candy Bishop and I am an active member of a Satanic cult known as Souls for Satan. You don't have to join if you take over my slave Steve but there would be a lot of advantages. Let me explain more. Souls for Satan is very much into breaking up marriages, all kinds of sexual perversion, making wives into adulteresses and prostitutes, all for heavy sadistic satisfaction. We pose as a 'swing club' for members only, we have 'swing parties' and offer marriage counselling to new swinging couples. We encourage the wife to be very promiscuous and drain the husband dry of all cash. We have a 75% success rate and good lawyers and dissolve marriages permanently.

In Steve's case it was classic: his wife did not really want to swing. Steve talked her into coming to us for 'counselling', for beginning swingers. She only went along because she loved him and he persisted. We talked to Penny, his wife, for several hours and convinced her it would help her marriage to do what Steve wanted. They had been married ten years and neither one had ever been unfaithful. Also Penny had been a virgin when she married Steve and had never had another man. I knew we could turn her over fast as that, and we did. Steve paid me $2,000 for the privilege of joining our club and all I did was help his sexy, loyal wife get fucked.

Because Penny was very nervous, I suggested they swing separately at first. We were very happy when they agreed to that. I had them agree also that for one whole month they wouldn't have sex with each other, but only with other people, and they could talk about what happened, and at the end of the month they could get together with their favourites. I told Steve privately since Penny was so inexperienced it was going to take awhile for her to get broken in. All her sex at first would be from other men, I told him this was how it went, and he agreed to everything.

I told Steve during the first week that Penny was swinging with a different guy every night that the girls I had lined up for him were sick, out of town, pregnant, and to bear with me. I really had no intention of getting him any dates at all.

I helped Penny the first time. We went shopping for sexy clothes, tear-away blouses, push-up bras and garter belts. She had high-heels with ankle straps, and I put her in exotic heavy make-up and a whorish hair-do and dye-job. When Steve saw how I had changed her he was all turned on and couldn't wait for the month to be over. That first night when I came to pick her up for her first date I could see Steve was jealous and wondering what he was doing. I told him Penny might be gone all night. I introduced her to a handsome body-building stud we pay to break the women in. He did things to her she couldn't believe. I wanted her to get good and addicted to wild sex, very different from what she was used to with Steve.

When I got home there were a dozen messages on my answering machine from Steve practically crying and begging me to get him a date. I didn't call him back. In the morning I went back over to their house, it was after twelve and Penny still hadn't come home. I was very happy. As the month went on Penny fucked over twenty men. All my regulars liked her a lot and I made a nice stack of cash. None of them told her they were paying for it, of course. The men in the coven didn't pay of course but made her do all kinds of perverted, freaky things. In all their years of marriage Steve had never had anal sex with Penny. When she finally did, it was with another man. When Penny told him about it he got mad at last and called her a whore. He was mad at me too because he wasn't getting any dates, but Penny ran to me to hide when Steve started breaking up the house. I sent some heavy-duty types over the next day, as friends of Penny's, to pack up her stuff and move her out while he was at work. Steve called us up crying and we had a good laugh. Penny's personality had changed, she was more aggressive and happy. Everything was working out great.

A few weeks later I went over to see Steve and told him I was sorry the swinging hadn't worked out right. I started doing stuff to him that I knew he liked, because Penny told me. I was playing with his nipples and staring him in the eyes, wearing a low-cut blouse. I told him we were moving into the next phase and now women were going to be coming over, but not to do what *he* wanted. He was going to have to do what they wanted. Actually there were no women, it was just going to be me. Penny got me a key to the house and I walked in any time I wanted, day or night, teased him and played with him. I told him if he passed the test he could have his wife back. We got Steve to sign papers giving Penny the house, and he had to move out.

One thing I did which really put Steve in our pocket was I brought over a video-tape of his wife getting fucked. She was really enjoying it with two guys at once, getting pumped and used and come all over and really loving it. While he was watching this video I told him, Penny wanted you to have this, and I put a framed wedding-photo of himself and Penny on top of the television. So he sat there watching his wife with other men moaning and bouncing, while the wedding-photo of his loving sweetheart smiled at him. I was having a ball taking out his mind and playing with it.

I have started getting Steve into bondage and torturing him, I whipped him with an extension cord and left welts all over him, I have stuck straight pins into his ass all the way to the head. But I need help from a professional to torture him better. He still has a lot of stocks to cash in, and property to sell. To show you how we worked him he signed over a $300,000 house to his wife without a peep. She gave the Coven 10% for helping her get out of her boring marriage. She also gave me some expensive gifts for letting her live with me and helping her meet all the studs.

Just to show you how far she has come, I went away for a month and told her to try to fuck as many strange men as she could. I told her to ask them for some money, for groceries, or whatever. She seemed to think this would be fun, and when I got back I was thrilled to know she had fucked the mailman, the manager of the supermarket, the delivery boys, the telephone repairman, some cops, the pump-jockeys at the gas station, a bunch of construction workers down the block, and a few door-to-door salesmen. She made over a thousand dollars. Not bad for a woman who was a loyal wife only a few months ago.

I have told Steve he is still going to have to go through an enormous amount of torture, before his wife will see him again. I told him to write to his wife, long letters he wrote that must have taken days to finish. Of course she never wrote back to him because I threw the letters away after picking through them for details about how to torture him better. She knew nothing about the letters and Steve was devastated because she never answered. What a ball!

The Mistress who will take Steve on has to really be able to enjoy this torture and mind-fuck and do it all for her own pleasure. I am hoping to find someone who is experienced in sticking surgical needles into penis and nipples and applying electro-shock. I really want him even more fucked up than he is now. He has a business that makes good money and you could make a permanent situation for yourself. I hope you will be as strict as I am when it comes to sex. I have never let Steve jack off in front of me ever, I hope you are a real Mistress and don't give him anything, no relief at all. Have no mercy on him in any way, take him and leave him living in a dive motel, totally broke.

I enclose a document drawn up by my attorney, giving you total freedom to do whatever you want with Steve. This attorney is very good, this contract is legally binding. If you get tired of Steve you can even kill him, and if you're caught this contract will get you out of having to go to jail. Believe me! Tease him wearing sexy exotic make-up, long fingernails, tight nylon hose held up by garters, and the highest heels you can find. Torture his nipples gently for hours and his mind turns into pudding and he will sign any check.

I do feel bad I can't continue to do him in myself. It would be so much fun, but I want to do other things for a while and travel. It would be such a shame to let all my good work go to waste, he should not be let free where he could go and get a divorce and forget about Penny and remarry. I enclose his photo, and S.A.S.E. with his address. Write to him. I showed him your picture in the magazine and he is expecting a letter from you.

From the day Steve and Penny walked into my house for 'swingers counselling' Steve has not had sex with a woman. I have made sure he never goes anywhere since his wife left him. He has not had any sex in almost a year now. Have no mercy on him in any way. Work him good. If you need to write to me, Candy Bishop, do so in care of my lawyer, Cody Brown. Just put the letters 'CB' for Candy Bishop in the left-hand bottom corner, and he will forward it to me without opening it. Good luck. Get to work on him, you will never regret it. Really fuck him over.

Love, Candy

Steve Dann   Cody Brown
Todd Motel   6662 Randolph Street
2337 Ventura Avenue   Riverside, California
Riverside, California

"Contract"

I Steve Dann being of sound mind hereby give my body to my Mistress _____. As part of my total slavery I expect great physical pain and/or damage to my body. It is my expectation to accept any action of my Mistress and hold her in no way liable for any permanent physical damage. Money may be taken from Steve Dann by my Mistress for any reason whatsoever, and everything he has is hers with no recourse. This document cannot be amended or cancelled. It is with Steve Dann's free will that any physical damage is solely at Steve Dann's request and can be done in any way his Mistress sees fit. This being Steve Dann's strong religious belief and his freedom according to the Constitution of the United States of America to worship as he pleases, also holding to his rights under the separation of church and state.

This document holds that the physical pain BE PERFORMED. It is a document of action, and written for the sole purpose of that PAIN BEING FULFILLED! The physical damage, pain and torture will go on for an extended period of time, without Steve Dann being able to make any determination as to that length and all action taking place having NO LIMITS.

Signed, Steve Dann

Witnesses signature, Cody Brown, Attorney at Law

This nauseating letter is but one scrap of the detritus of unfathomable human suffering daily crossing the Desk of Angel Stern. The sad, demented soul who penned it is of course the hapless knucklehead 'Steve Dann', who might be no more than a clerk in the law office of 'Cody Brown', where he might intercept choice letters to that infamous Sataness 'Candy Bishop' – the strange violent character he has invented to console himself in his obviously living hell of a life. 'Candy' takes from him any responsibility he might have for his wife 'Penny' leaving him flat. That he might be a pervert, a degenerated masochist, and sadistically pimped his wife in swing clubs is not the real story, in this fantasy: Satan is the one who made all the bad things happen.

That he had a wife who did leave him we may confidently assume. He is no doubt one of the poor, naive, middle-class losers who still believe that 'swinging' is the groovy cure for the bored marriage-bed. Not being able to stand the idea that his wife might have left him after sampling a rampant stud, he has created Candy Bishop as the excuse for his current victim-status. This Satanic sorceress changed his wife's personality – made her 'more aggressive and happier' (interesting criticism) – transformed her into a whore whom he however cannot buy! Very likely the original for Candy is some friend of his wife's, around during the break-up, who perhaps got her a date or two. Friends who help at such troubled times are usually loathed, and accused of everything from lying to brain-washing to satanic wiles.

Steve Dann is sadistic – any man who dangles his wife in the cess-pools of 'swingdom' is that – but his masochism is of course more pronounced. Hence his call for the 'professional' who can torture him properly, take him out of the misery of his solitary self-beatings with extension cords. To jam a puny inch of pin into the massy thick muscles of the *gluteus maximus* is not an astonishing feat for a pain-addict: he wants, and needs much more. Somehow I can't imagine a real Sataness admitting she doesn't know how to inflict more pain on a willing schlump like Steve.

The two signatures on the pitiful contract are identical. The poor lunk merely switched pens to sign the two names, as if that would trick anyone. He is obviously hoping to receive two letters from each respondent: one lying, cajoling, seductive one to 'Steve', and a more brazen satanic one, revealing all vile motives, to 'Candy'. He could thus be confirmed in his fantasy that Satanic women do exist. I myself of course never responded. Within a couple of weeks I did receive a letter from 'Steve' himself, begging me to please consider his application. He enclosed with his letter a key, supposedly to his house, with a map on how to find him in the suburbs. The real 'key' to this fantasy is in the reversal of every statement of Candy's. Attribute her violent attitude to the same person of Steve and you have a clear reading on a commonplace but nonetheless pathetic tragedy of modern married life.

Steve wishes to be finished off, ruined financially, so that he may at last be left in peace: thus Candy's command, "Take him and leave him in a dive motel, totally broke." Given Steve's address we might gather that he is already thus reduced. "You can even kill him," says Candy – he wishes he were dead. "The contract will get you out of going to jail" – if he kills himself, he won't have to go be tormented any more.

Candy embodies the sadistic side of Steve, reflecting his probably early point of view. His wife changed her appearance, no doubt under his own urging. He'd never seen her look so good – sexy violence done to a loyal and loving wife. But no 'swinging' husband ever plans for his wife to run off, after finding out in bed about 'things... she could not believe'. Candy says, "I really had no intention of getting (Steve) any dates at all." That is, Steve could not follow through on the swinging dates he might have actually had, perhaps being impotent. When Penny ran away Candy says, "(Steve) was mad at me too, because he wasn't getting any dates." That is, Steve was mad at himself because his wife could swing, and he could not. Later, when more mean manipulations are planned for Steve, Candy says, after telling Steve dominant women were going to come and use him, "Actually there were no women – it was just going to be me." That is, there would be no more women in his life – he was masturbating alone.

An almost sweet, sad twist to the fantasy, that his wife has been made a prostitute, is that Steve 'keeps her' unknowledgable of this dealing. In this way he can imagine she is still almost pure. These men his dear wife entertains are liars, users; they don't love her and appreciate her, as he had. But while he left-handedly pities her for this exploitation, he is still sadistically pimping her. He degrades whatever pleasure she may be feeling, places her in the most exploitative situation a woman could be in, does not let her enjoy the cash she is so happily earning. However at the same time Steve is himself a 'john', tolerated only for his cash-value. And although he pays and pays, he still ends up with nothing, dry-hustled by the evil machinations of the Sataness Candy.

So he sits alone, a masochist dupe, filled with self-torment, unable to fight back. He is the pawn of a coven of cruelly laughing women, who use their powers to milk him dry. He will eventually be killed – if only that day would come sooner! "The physical damage, pain and torture will go on for an extended period of time without Steve Dann being able to make any determinations as to that length, and all action taking place having NO LIMITS." This is as in the play by Sartre, *No Exit*, where all action takes place in a locked cell in Hell, every person trapped in a repetitive round of torment for all eternity. The horror of the play is the confrontation with a truth that cannot ever be escaped. One is doomed to be conscious forever, turning over and replaying an error without the possibility of an instant's rest. We see Steve in the hell that is the private playground of the confirmed masochist. Punished by Satan, he never leaves his shabby motel-room, bound to the constant punishment and torment of his new status: slave. He mails his room-key to strange women in the hope that perhaps some psychopathic type will find him, creep in, and hurt him in a way he has yet to imagine. Anything would be better than the same old pain. Anything better than thinking these same thoughts, going over and over his crimes against his wife. Anything is better than these old porno videos, where the woman who resembles his wife, the whore, is fucked again and again as he stares at their wedding photo propped up atop the television. We can imagine he has been compelled to give her everything she has asked for – lest it come out in court that along with his pimping her through swing-clubs, he asked her to inflict pain, and even 'permanent damage'. Of course to lose one's house and savings could be classified as that, but it is I am sure not what Steve had in mind.

"It would be such a shame to let him go free," translates to, "Keep me in this maudlin slough, where I can continue to blame Satanic control, where I can go on longing for my wife whom I still love, and thankfully die in the grip of some ultimate cruelty, imposed from without, to save me from the fearful act of doing it myself."

Strange slavey men who send unknown violent women their house-keys would appear to be eager to destroyed. But I had the idea this was all the hoax of some chronic stay-at-home, who was sending out his next-door neighbour's address and perhaps their key that had been unwittingly entrusted to him. This bathrobe jockey, bored out of his mind, was praying he might see fantastic exotic women arriving in droves, marching in teetering heels to hammer on the door and shout in terrifying voices that they had arrived, ready and willing to inflict the 'permanent damage'.

Dear Steve, if only there could be for you some merciful Satanic cult to take you over. Damn that free will, anyway. We wish we could find you the antidotal incantation that would break the spell and bring your loving wife home again. It is so soothing to consider that you were lied to, conspired against, used... that your wife never saw any of your letters, because that awful woman threw them away. Better think that, than imagine she read them and never bothered to answer. Penny was torn from you by forces beyond your control. You are not to blame, she is not to blame. Satan is a kind of natural disaster, more than human, like a typhoon. Satan is the one who broke your life to ruins, Satan makes you wallow in front of the TV. Satan took your wife away to be used by the terrible, virile men – while you are abandoned to a marginal subsistence as a lonely pervert.

fantasy of divine right: randy #222, aka prince thornton of dagmalvia

We shall commence this interesting case with a press release concerning "The Prince":

About The Prince:
Prince Thornton of Dagmalvia (shown here in a photograph some years old, outside the Royal Dagmalvian Palace) is the sole heir to the Dagmalvian throne. As the Communists currently overrun Dagmalvia, in their nasty dirty uniforms and cheap Soviet shoes, The Prince has been forced to defect to the United States, lest he be murdered by the filthy illiterate bastards. He has lost his kingdom, his fortune – but not his throne! He lives at an undisclosed location in Manhattan. The days of sleek Italian sports-cars are over. While photographs of The Prince at lavish society-parties may adorn from time to time the rear pages of Vanity Fair, he can no longer know the pleasure of having Dagmalvian debutantes fighting over him, grovelling at his feet for a sniff at his wealth and grandeur. Nor can he any longer enjoy those abuses it is still widely rumoured he inflicted with impunity upon certain of his favourites.

In Manhattan, only Doctor Angel Stern, Psychiatrist to the Royal European families, knows his true whereabouts at any time. This eloquent doctor has taken him into her care. He is totally dependent upon her to help see him through his current plight. It is rumoured in some of the lower circles of downtown society that she is inducting him into the further arcana of sexual abuse that he himself not so long ago practised upon his serfs and serf-maidens. We feel certain of Dr. Stern's powers to aid in his positive assimilation into the modern, corrupt world of democracy.

The writer of this 'press release' is Slave Randy #222, 'Prince Thornton' of the invented European sovereignty of 'Dagmalvia'. Though he was for us for many years yet another client with a complex and pronounced taste for humiliation, I came to know well another side: a sadistic, arrogant, overweening ego, parading itself as a 'royal' self. In general he does comport himself with the air of an upper-class snob, nose in the air, a feeble type of nervous tweedy intellectual, impertinent, presumptuous and caustic. His personality is subject to marked and rapid changes, ricochetting from a profound submissive masochism to an insufferable hauteur. He is volatile, and as may be derived from the accounts he had given me of his former psychoanalyses, has even proved himself to be 'dangerous', to the point of having been placed for a time on a psychiatrists' blacklist (an internal reference for the profession). That the therapist who thus reported him as 'committable' was a young and terrified female does not seem so odd; but we of course know the other side of The Prince – the one whom we depose – the one we tear from his protective bed of royalty – the humiliated clown we always keep down.

Ten years ago when we first met Randy he was known as 'Randy the Pie-Man', an innocuous title based on his fetish for enjoying meringue pies scuffed in his face. We knew little of him but that he was a completely satisfying submissive. Over the years he developed his fetishism, and to pie Randy properly required a bakery-full of coconut cream, key-lime, Boston custard-cream, lemon meringue and chocolate cream pie. (He enjoys reciting these flavours aloud, and includes their names in all correspondence.) Also to be found in the humiliating ammunition are cans of whipped cream, chocolate syrup, black-strap molasses, canned pie-filling in cherry and blueberry, maple syrup and of course maraschino cherries – all of which is slathered over his writhing, ecstatic and fully-dressed body.

Here follows one evening's "programme" for his session, as always minutely detailed and mapped out in 10-minute increments.

"Dear Mistress Angel,

It is so exciting to see you again as it has been a long time. If you recall I find being embarrassed and laughed at most erotic. Please do not be afraid to show amusement. I also prefer to remain in costume throughout the session, except, of course, when my pants are taken away. Is it possible for you to take on the appearance of a college co-ed, with sweater-set, pearls, and flats? Thanking you in advance, I remain, sincerely, Prince Thornton.

P.S. I hope it was not presumptuous of me to have had the groceries delivered to you. I hope it did not inconvenience you in any way. It is a lot for The Prince to carry."

Randy always varied his context, placing The Prince in one embarrassing predicament after another. In this special manifestation, he was a freshman 'pledge' for a fraternity, which had assigned The Prince to their sister sorority, to make certain his pledging-trial would be greatly difficult. In the scenario's outline he clarified 'motives' for us, the 'reason' for his torment:

*"The fraternity has no intention of going through with my initiation. They wish only to deliberately and outrageously degrade and embarrass me. Particularly before the eyes of the Sorority, which should be easy, as I am a Nerd (that is of the **highest** intelligence which in this disgusting culture has only a **pathetic** status)."*

This first meeting with the Sorority Sisters took place in an imaginary abandoned warehouse, far off-campus, away from the ears of the campus-police who might hear his blood-curdling shrieks for mercy. He had been instructed to dress as for a party, and indeed he arrived for his session in a silly tuxedo, pastel brocade with a matching cummerbund, patent leather shoes rounding out the picture. I and my two friends, in sweater-sets and pearls, garters and high heels, have been assigned by our frat-boyfriends the task of 'really doing in the Nerd'.

"Please begin by introducing yourselves and telling me what hell I am going to be put through and what a good time you are going to milk out of me. You find it so amusing to have a man totally in your power, especially the disgusting snob, antiquated piece-of-shit, left-over scrap of royalty I am.

Demand that I pull down my trousers and present myself to you with them around my ankles. Comment on the state of my undershorts. Insist that I hand my trousers over to you – I will have to comply with your every demand, otherwise I will never get them back. Of course you and your friends are so beautiful I do this instantly, thinking it is a prelude to sex. Instead I am bent over in a rude, exposed, public way for a prolonged paddling. Being college-girls you won't be so brazen as to expose my naked buttocks. Tell me how you would enjoy raping me, how you're going to let your fraternity boyfriends fuck me. Recite the names as you insult me so: faggot, cocksucker, pussy, sissy, nerd."

After this humiliating softening, Randy is led to a plastic drop-cloth and given back his pants – for he must be totally dressed for his final ruination. Beginning with a slow trickle of chocolate syrup through his hair, we take up our pies and descend upon him, screaming with joy as the first pie soils his face. As his pants are filled with whipped cream, his hair massaged with molasses, the warp and woof of his costume gummed up with the glutinous mass, our laughter becomes more sarcastic, more cruel. Now slaps in the face are administered, kicks, real violence is done to him; he is thus terrorized into thanking us for his total humiliation.

"6 lemon meringue pies, 6 small key-lime pies, 6 cans of whipped cream, 2 cans blueberry pie-filling, 1 large jar U-Bet chocolate syrup, 1 squirt-jar Hershey's syrup, 1 jar Karo dark corn syrup, 1 bottle Grandma's black-strap molasses.

Please do not be afraid to ruin all my clothes and totally pollute my hair. After I am forced to masturbate at the end of the session, allow me to leave, covered with the pie et al, to walk all the way home thus attired, exposed to the derision of the public at large."

Terence Sellers

Yet with Randy there was always the thought there might come a day when the Nerd would have his revenge... and this idea obtruded into reality the day I received the call where he told me of his rejection by his psychiatrist, and her blacklisting him.

His story of the reason behind the inspiring moment of his rejection was such: yes, he had been pissed off at this doctor, fed up with her 'weakling attempts to make (him) conform to a "norm"'; yes, he had called her repeatedly on the telephone, often saying nothing; yes, he had broken into her answering-machine's privacy code, listened to her private messages, and enjoyed her look of puzzlement when he revealed the knowledge he had stolen (for neither had she ever received said calls, for as well he could erase all her messages); yes, he had gone to her apartment in the middle of the night on several occasions, rung the doorbell, and run away. But worse than any of this was the day he pretended to be nice. Sitting in her waiting-room, he availed himself of the coffee-machine, and brought his doctor a nice cup of coffee... into which he had masturbated, right there in the waiting-room, with no doors locked to hide his crime. Through the session he happily watched her sip the coffee to the last drop. But that wasn't enough. He could not constrain his joy, needed to see her answering horror. Now we shall never know if Randy actually did this filthy deed, but the point is the doctor became enraged – probably understanding that he is *fully* capable of it! If I had been his doctor then, I would have pretended I didn't believe him, stripped him and whipped him soundly for inventing such nastiness, then gone on with the regular therapy, (not before making myself vomit). But then I am of course more versatile than the average therapist.

For all his bravado Randy was agonized by the ostracism. The authoritarian proscription against him as a proper patient effectively shut the door against his receiving conventional therapy. Dismissed from the ranks of the good little neurotics, he could only turn to me, who could certainly handle the bad, evil and dangerous ones. To be classified in some mysterious psychiatric log as 'dangerous' is certainly to risk incarceration. Indeed one doctor he tried to make an appointment with suggested that The Prince commit himself! As one of Randy's most serious fetishes is for psychoanalysis, one may imagine the trauma he underwent. I assured him I would undertake his analysis, as well as continuing to act out with The Prince.

But why was our Prince in therapy at all? Aside from the usual childhood traumata, at an early age abused by family, psychically castrated, *et cetera*, an etiology we observe in nearly all these cases, he had recently had yet another unhappy love-affair. He revealed to me that the object of his attentions had been none other than my associate Mistress Helga Lamaze, aka Jane. They had not engaged in sex but had known the peculiarly awful sort of attachment, so rife with torment, that is to be had between two sadomasochists of high degree. But even Jane's masochism was not so twisted as to tolerate the violent threat The Prince soon presented to her everyday life.

Mistress Helga had been so 'seduced' by his winning personality and funny fetish that she consented to date him – a grievous error. As in psychiatry there is that restriction placed upon the parameters of the doctor-patient relationship, so have we always avoided the possibility that a client might mistake us for a girlfriend – which they easily do, even after one dinner-date. I understood this to be particularly important in the case of Prince Thornton, for whom the lines between fantasy and reality were not blackly drawn. Happy little Pie-Man, harbouring a tyrant within, who patiently awaits the moment when he can enjoy his secret pleasure – to top the 'Top', and thus void the dominating control. He showed me photographs she had allowed him to take – there she was, in a park, wearing shorts and pigtails, laughing on a swing! Needless to say I was horrified. What a strange case of the Two Abnormals, under the spell of 'normality' – oh no, he didn't need control, and no – she didn't have to keep him under control! Silly bliss! with painful consequences.

When the lady in question became engaged and refused to see The Prince any longer, he discovered that he had quite fallen in love with her. Hence his return to therapy as he felt himself close to having a nervous breakdown. Now The Prince could rage against her, and plan revenge, and did so quite openly with me, stating firmly that the only satisfaction he might now have was to be able to kill her with his bare hands. Certainly as I knew the lady in question and had known her to act without conscience before. I acknowledged to him her abuse of his submissiveness – to play as she had as a 'girlfriend' was to go beyond his ordinary capacity for humiliation. She had wakened the vengeful Prince and now it was my responsibility to bring him back to heel.

Randy/Thornton called Jane/Helga constantly, often saying nothing. He began to stalk her, waiting outside her apartment or the Dungeon, sometimes saying nothing, oftimes making some sarcastic comment. He was invariably dressed as The Prince for this, that is, nattily, in tie and cuff-links, sometimes in his ceremonial attire – a military-style 'uniform' with gold braid, epaulettes, and phoney decorations. This costuming terrorized Helga/Jane more than anything. I requested he desist from the stalking, as it made him look ridiculous and opened him to police action. He snickered and snarled over the stupidity of marrying, procreating, becoming a housewife. "For her to marry that idiot – such a degradation – such a downfall." Well Randy aren't such things a part of life? What if she had married you? "She would never have had to do anything – not a dish – lift a finger – nothing. She could have sat on satin pillows all day long!" The Prince was suffering gravely from the loss of his Ideal. "How can you marry... a waiter?" he screamed at her over the telephone.

Jane had also been so thoughtless as to let Randy know where her fiancé worked. The Prince began to haunt the place, going in and sitting over a cup of coffee for hours, glaring. Jane was apprised of it when The Prince called to laugh, "He looks so cute in his apron – I left him a nickel for a tip!" When at last the fiancé confronted Randy, with aplomb The Prince invited him to sit and "discuss the REAL Jane". For Jane's lover this was just another reason for her to quit forever the business of slaving. I insisted he immediately quit his stalking or I too would reject him from therapy. As I had the advantage of hearing both sides, I let Randy frankly know they considered him sad and absurd. "They're not at all frightened – if that's what you wanted." This seemed to make a strong impression and he promised me to desist from this grossest form of his obsession.

I wanted to know of course what had been the conditions of his former rejections by other women. "As soon as they get to know The Prince – they get scared and want to get away." I began to understand that The Prince Thornton of Dagmalvia was his form of the Superior – a man who embodied the most powerful idea of himself – royalty deposed, a shining star in the mud, a creature imbued with Divine Right that we in this degraded mass-society can no longer recognize, much less understand and kneel to. More and more of The Prince's underground machinations to re-attain his power were revealed to me, as he waxed violent over Helga.

"If only I could kill a woman – Jane would of course be my preferred victim – but I think any woman would do, now."

"But won't you just need to kill another one, after that? Isn't that usually the case with sex-murder – like a chicken-killing dog, once you get that heady scent of blood in your nostrils...?"

"No – *I* would only have to do it *once.*"

"There is no way to know that. What if you discovered you'd have to do it again – and again? What a life – and you'd eventually be caught."

"Well, you don't know that."

"You would have to confess. You have a conscience – it would torture you. You'd want the world to know, anyway. Is that the future you see for yourself – locked in a cell, reviled as a monster?"

"Of course you have to say all this. What else could you say, Doctor – 'I'll set it up for you – I know a suicidal girl'?"

I asserted that just because I was a kind of radical psychologist and a dominatrix, apparently inured to every nightmare of behaviour, did not mean I could tolerate any and all peculiarities. I had limits too. I told him he must accept the fact that all his emotions would be more passionate, his feelings always excessive – beyond the limits of the average person. He seemed interested to hear this theory I have developed – that the masochist is particularly more sensitive and gifted with an expansive range of feelings. They do suffer more, and the suffering has more dimension. I understood that this idea would enamour The Prince, who is always interested in whatever raises him above the common herd.

"As a result of your supersensitivity, you must more stringently *protect yourself* and refuse to have anything to do with unlawful abusers, the blindly cruel, the normal and thick-skinned."

I assured him I appreciated his rage. Many masochists and/or submissives dream of marrying a truly dominant person. To have no more secrets – to be able to express *all* – to no longer be pariah, but accepted and loved for what they are – perhaps even 'cured' of their strangeness by their great love! But now that fantasy was over. There was no great love – there would be no magical 'cure'. He was thrown back upon himself as a loathsome and rejected pervert. Treated dismissively by her *waiter fiancé* – intolerable! He was The Prince, such things were not done! The Prince was the axle that turned him back to his consolation – his Divine Right – to punish the peons, jail the disrespectful, put them all in their places – underground, if necessary!

I persisted in questioning him as to his desire to kill a woman. He responded to my interest, especially the question that I myself had once been asked by a therapist: If you were to kill someone, how would you do it? Now it was his turn to retract, admit that his sadistic bent had been shamblingly at fault. We agreed he had to have an outlet. Like some Raskolnikov he was sedentary, melancholic, brooding at home when he was not out stalking, or wandering aimlessly, or making his funny phone-calls. I insisted he at least use his talent, his well-evolved ability to invent, project, fantasize and act out trauma – and achieve what satisfaction there was within it – *to find the pleasure in this new pain, in order to cathect it.*

I did admit this was so far problematic. No longer could I offer the conciliatory pacifying reversals of his former masochism. But I did firmly believe he could get out of his torturous entanglements through a psychodrama. I considered that he might come to me and pretend he had killed someone – and to make to me the full confession. As a sort of dangerous inversion of Jung's active imagination, we would enter upon the fantasies of a crime, and follow every twisting path of its possibility.

"I could be the judge to whom you make the full confession." He said he would think about it. "Then we could have the trial, and you might confess to us all – to a whole audience of women." This did not render him enthusiastic.

As his sadistic fantasies continued, I did begin to receive a number of hang-up calls, very late, and my doorbell was rung a few times, to no issue. But I never let The Prince know I suspected him of this. (Anyhow it might have been any one of a number of psychopaths.) Then, all at once, came a whole new outpouring of Dagmalvian elaborations. The royal violence was waxing most immense, and was so forbidden – by our debased democratic morality? – that it required an answering violence on the part of the female authorities.

"Dear Dr. Stern:

You have read the papers – the communist takeover of Dagmalvia is complete. The situation for myself and what is left of my family is desperate. I am on the lam again, and without funds. I have hit bottom, I need to see you, but I can barely find enough money for food.

I confess, in order to gain some money I have taken employment as a male escort – a horror of a situation for someone like myself. It is a very exclusive, all-male heterosexual agency on East 64th Street. All had been going well, and I was economically surviving on my knees licking grey-haired pussy for some weeks when one evening it happened. I was sent on a call to the Pierre to entertain two women – I was going to be paid double. I was no sooner in the room than the women announced I was under arrest for prostitution. I tried to explain my position in the Royal Family and the desperation to which I had been driven, but they only revelled in this information. They stripped me to my underwear and made me perform for them, as they commanded, or they would take me in, call reporters, and reveal all. They abused me for hours. My clothing was thrown out onto Fifth Avenue. I was handcuffed to the bed while the two of them took turns sitting on my face, turning me over and sodomising me with the high-heels of their shoes, in the most vicious manner possible.

They tried to force a champagne bottle into my rectum, gagging me with a washcloth. They tortured me with lit cigarettes on my testicles, dragged me into the bathroom and held my head in the used toilet-bowl water until I confessed the information they needed concerning my Dagmalvian bank accounts. It turned out they were not really undercover policewomen but agents of a European terrorist group known only as THE ORGANISATION. They led me out of the Pierre wearing only a t-shirt, shorts, my black socks and shoes, and of course my Royal sock-garters with the Royal Crest emblazoned on the sides for all to see.

I am broke again after paying their bribes, but I need to see you. I feel it would be invaluable. As you know Dr. Stern you are the only psychiatrist in New York that is of the quality to treat The Prince. I would be glad to provide you with a multitude of services in exchange for therapy. I would be happy to provide a humiliating entertainment for any of your lady-friends at Xmas-time, say, I could ring their bell and do a humiliating strip-tease. Or in the guise of 'performance art', have shit smeared on my face on a stage at a local underground nightclub. Or I could report with a lemon meringue pie when, where and to whomever you like. I could pie someone for you, or merely report with the pie, and offer myself as target. Or if you would like me to, serve you as a menial. Should you be gracious enough to grant me a therapy session, I promise to follow any directive. You are the expert.

Sincerely yours,

Prince Thornton,
His Royal Highness Of Dagmalvia"

We spoke frequently on the telephone, and he would come from time to time to my office for the 'talking-cure'. During the year that we continued at this level his rage against Helga/Jane rarely abated. But The Prince was ever embroiled in new and degrading adventures that had taken a decided turn away from cruel co-eds or sneering communists. He would now be the sexual servant to the class of criminal Negro men. While he continued to insist that he did not hate women, that he was not in any way a homosexual, that he would never have an affair with a man, he did not deny that he had become addicted to a black-male-chat-line: he called these strange men every night, and paid to hear them tell him what they would do if they ever got their hands on little 'whitey'. The Prince 'knew' that these men were 'the most violent in the world'. He understood 'how easy' it was for them to 'totally lose control' and kill him. We see here the twist on his wish that he might also, easily, lose all control.

Randy thus evolved the fantasy that would appease his own violence. His former thought-crime – desiring to kill – had been inverted to the fantasy that he was to be the recipient of a murderous caress. The logic ran, "Since I wanted to kill a woman, I myself will be killed." Or better still, "Since I can't kill a woman, I'd rather be dead."

He called me up one evening half-hysterical, telling me that one of the black men was on his way – coming over to The Prince's apartment.

"Why did you give him your address, you fool?!"
"I didn't – he got it out of the call-service-files!"
"Well, call the agency!"

I tried to help him cope. But as he continued on the fact that the doorbell would ring, was that the doorbell, was someone knocking... the man was coming up to kill him, I understood The Prince was deep in fantasy. Something about that doorbell, as a prelude to violence?... I realized he was enjoying illicit phone-sex with me!

Later, he arranged for his best friend – who happens to be a homosexual – to come with him to a hotel room, and be with him when the Negro call-boy arrived. The friend then took a number of high-quality, detailed photographs of The Prince in his ceremonial uniform on his knees performing fellatio. These incriminating images were mailed to me with the following letter:

"Dear Most Cruel and Villainous Dr. Stern:

As you may already know, the Royal Prince Thornton of Dagmalvia has become a thorn in the side of THE ORGANISATION, as we continue to aid the Revolution in the backward monarchist state of Dagmalvia. He refuses to accept the deep responsibility he has towards his people and country, and remains a degenerate expatriate in your country. We intensely dislike his conceited, arrogant high profile as he exhibits himself in the decadent high-society of Manhattan. We are tired of seeing photographs of this fascist in the likes of Details and Vanity Fair magazines. Snob poseur extraordinaire, who robbed the country's coffers before jetting off to be photographed at lavish parties with his nose in the air. We ask your help in psychologically breaking him down to recognize his crimes, and we intend to spend the rest of our lives tormenting him to establish our message to the world!

At this moment we have The Prince locked in a cell on the Lower East Side. He has been fed crusts and water when we bother to ungag his dirty mouth. His debauched lifestyle was indeed his downfall – imagine how easy it was for us to take him out of a nightclub VIP lounge, where he lay supine soaked to the gills in fine cognac! He will be released only if you agree to come here and let us watch you have your full sadistic way with him, the way we know you are capable of. Enough of this claptrap psychoanalyzing. He does not know where he is, who has abducted him – he does not even know who you really are!

We request that you dress in the most conventional way, as if you were one of those women The Prince sees socially: black sheath, pearls, beige stockings and low-heeled shoes. Should you wish to act on any personal sadistic impulse while we have The Prince in our grasp we give it our full approval. It is no use trying to help such a parasitical monster as he is, any longer. An expert psychologist such as yourself should recognize that only punitive incarceration will serve him as he deserves.

We look forward to meeting you.

THE ORGANISATION

P.S. You may see from the enclosed photographs that we have already begun making him pay back the money he has stolen. We have placed the price of three dollars upon a congress with him, thus providing sexual relief to an underprivileged group, so he is forced, for the first time in his life, to behave in a socially responsible manner."

After I received this notice, I telephoned to determine exactly what it was The Prince now wanted. Did he wish to make an appointment, for a session of punishing imprisonment? Was he planning to bring the call-boy with him? He did not answer my calls, and from this missive there was no issue. For the first time I began to be irritated with his presuming upon me with his fantasies – in a way that was bringing little pleasure to me. Nor was I happy with my new designation, 'most cruel and villainous'. I saw how his mistreatment at the hands of his psychiatrist, and from Helga/Jane, was the source of the persecution he imagined himself to be receiving at the hands of the 'Organisation'. I did not want to be classified with this evil. I was sorry to imagine he might think 'it is no use trying any longer to help', or that I was the one understood that 'only punitive incarceration will serve him as he deserves'. I recognized Randy/Thornton as the victim of those who have absolutely no appreciation of Royalty – status-quo psychiatrists, for starters. Their purpose is not only to embarrass and degrade his experience, but to totally emasculate him, make him 'behave' as he never will behave. He is thrown amongst pariahs, though he too is one of the most violent of man – forced to serve those who ought 'by Divine Right' to be serving him.

Between the lines too I discerned he was perhaps taken up with some dissipation (fine cognac); was he now referring to his apartment (in the Lower East Side) as a cell? I was sadly struck by 'enough of this claptrap psychoanalyzing' – the letter held a tinge

of despair; of dissociation, anomie 'he does not know where he is...
he does not even know who you really are!' What was he trying to
say? For me this case was growing quite dispiriting, and I missed
our simple Randy Pieman. But in this catalytic conversion of trauma
to sex, one thing I have understood is no-one remains the same. In
the act of realizing it, the fantasy will always change. We see how
this was very true for the mercurial Prince.

After this dissatisfying exchange, I received, three days later, another
letter:

"Dear Dr. Stern:

*Just when I thought everything was going to go for the better! The
pitiful 'Organisation' lost their visas and are being deported back to
Dagmalvia (let them go ahead and impose their ridiculous
'government for the people' – what utter debasement!). I was doing
well as an escort, getting a lot of call-backs and regulars. I was
beginning to enjoy a regular income when the entire agency was
'busted'. It was my misfortune to be in the office collecting my pay
when the police arrived. My hands were cuffed behind me and I
was led out the front door to a waiting NYPD car. They brought me
to a place you Manhattanites call Riker's Island. I spent the
weekend in jail. During that time I became intimately acquainted
with your American Negro gentlemen.*

*I was placed in a cell with fourteen African-American gentlemen
who raped me repeatedly through the 60-odd hours I was there.
They maintained a very hostile and rude attitude about it I might
add. I was sodomised orally and anally countless times, was
urinated upon, and made too to swallow a great deal of it. At one
point while I was on my knees getting it 'royally', as they seem to
put it, a handful of human faeces was smeared across my face.*

*This is a very embarrassing story to relate to anyone, but I feel I
should talk to someone about it, so I am not further traumatised. I
trust you, as I know I can trust you not to find it amusing, as you
are a professional.*

My experiences with the communists, the police, the Negro gentlemen from the agency, and those at Riker's, the blackmail photos, I'm beginning to find it all quite taxing. Now I understand I am being blackmailed by one of the women clients. She threatens to tell the Press I am a whore. It seems no matter who I trust with the knowledge that I am The Prince, they always turn on me, always try to use me for their profit."

Again, no issue from this letter – only a frantic call a week later, demanding all his letters and photographs back. I assured him he could have them anytime, but there was no need to fear I would ever blackmail him. Then, all at once, Randy told me he was going to have to give up The Prince. I asked him why, and he said The Prince was leading him further on than he wished to go. But what had The Prince been invented for but to serve his greatest wish: to be with a woman also royal, to have a true love-affair. I observed that the greatest problem before us then was not to get rid of The Prince, but how to turn The Prince into a true Royal, restore him to his throne. He must become a benevolent ruler, not a tyrant that lays waste and terrorizes. Observe this impulse: you have to *scare* a woman. Why would you scare her away – if it were not for some purpose – perhaps under the agenda of homosexuality? He seemed quite struck by this and asked, "Yes – why? Why am I sending them away from me?"

At this point I may have embarrassed him intolerably with my idea that he was 'really' a homosexual. He stopped phoning and declared himself in no need of therapy. He was over his obsession with Helga/Jane – and thank you. I soon heard of him again, though, as he came to see Mistress Veronika in a completely new guise: he would be dressed, from head to toe, in an exquisite pink-and-white little girl's costume – with patent leather pumps, little white socks, and a bright pink pageboy wig with a bow atop. His face was made up like a whore's. I saw the photographs of his curtsey, his pirouette, and his genuflexion before Veronika – at her service. He was PRINCESS Rowena. No-one would ever pie *that* girl – she was too dainty – she was too good. This little travesty repeated itself a while, and then The Prince/Princess was gone again.

Terence Sellers

A year later, I heard from Randy briefly that he had found the help he really needed. His worst problem, it seemed, was not of a psychological nature, but that he was physically ill and weakened by a latent condition. This illness had caused the hysteria, the violence... this illness was the reason for the wild mood swings. We discovered he could indeed be calmer and quieter, as long as he followed his diet regimen and ingested a certain modern psychoactive drug daily. Before long The Prince had indeed fallen in love again, and even when his wife-to-be heard every Princely confession she did not find it in her heart to turn him away. The last thing I heard they had taken a honeymoon trip to Miami. But some things never change.

"Prince Thornton of Dagmalvia
Prince Thornton Hotel
Collins Avenue, Miami Beach

Dear Dr. Stern:

I may not return to New York. Last week while I was here in Miami you can see I won a lovely Art Deco hotel in a card game. My adolescence in Monte Carlo comes to my rescue now! The Cubans later however caught me cheating and what followed was a most wildly unpleasant experience. Don't worry, the doctors have assured me that my deadly good looks have not been damaged, and will return as soon as I heal.

Of course you and your associates are welcome to come down here and live whenever you like. Simply call the number on the enclosed card. Tell the concierge who answers that you are a personal friend of The Prince and to reserve the champagne suite with ocean-view. I have had installed a salt water pool that I am sure you will enjoy. Cut me slightly all over with a small knife and toss me in to amuse yourselves.

Best wishes,
Prince Thornton of Dagmalvia"

---

contract concerning the submission of dorian to mistress angel stern: a paradigm in six movements

London, August 27, 1990

Dear Mistress Angel,

I am that English client of yours who likes being squashed, sat upon, and crushed. You know I have longed for a very long session, yet I unpredictably change my mind and want to break away. Remember? For that reason I have spoken about wishing to sign a contract.

I am writing because I will be in New York the week of September 16th. I would like to stay at least twenty-four hours with you, and maybe Mistress Leila, as well as any friends you think appropriate. I would like to start preparing for it now!

I would be grateful if you could write to me and say which date you prefer, the 16th, 17th, or 19th. I am free all those evenings. Also so that I may psychologically prepare, an idea of what you may have in store; perhaps a copy of your contract, that I can read over and perhaps if it pleases you, add to; instruction as to what I should bring and hopefully photographs of yourself and Mistress Leila. I need to meditate continually in preparation. Warn me of every outrageous demand in your letter, plus those of your friends which are scarily unpredictable. My rebellious 'antibodies' will emerge, but I suspect I will accept your every demand. Consider not only our twenty-four fours, but the long term. My guess is that the more extreme and radical the warnings, the better, because that will give the antibodies time to work out, time will be on your side between the day I receive your letter and my arrival in New York. Imagine how much more significant my ringing your doorbell on the assigned day, when I know of all your outrageous designs, having been warned in advance, in writing! Imagine how much deeper my commitment to a contract I sign if I've had weeks to study it.

Outline your worst imaginings in the way of exploiting my fetish. If possible include photographs, you know full well that all the antibodies will be vanquished by the photos, by my overpowering longing to be crushed, squashed, sat on, stood on, lain upon, trampled and perhaps injured by those beautiful bodies, used by them as a couch, as they chat amongst themselves, forcing me under the mattress as they make passionate love, crushing me into the hard slats of the bed and perhaps suffocating me to death. How I long to be completely overpowered by those wholly superior bodies.

I know I have to pay for the privilege of being crushed; the next stage is I begin to rethink my dread of submitting to your whim. Is it not the will of the superior woman, owner of superior form and complex, terrifying mind? Is submitting to your whim only a cost, and not a privilege indeed? I submit thus in my mind, and am overcome with visions of what my life would be as your toy, victim, prisoner. However radical your proposals, the time available between my receipt of your letter, and the actual session will suffice to break down my antibodies to anything you should propose, the more radical the better, indeed I think a really radical and far-reaching letter from you will take me to the final, ultimate stage: from simply reading about your whims and thinking about them, to wanting them more than life itself and presenting my body before you as proof. But there is something even more than this that I desire – a longing for physical and metaphysical surrender of the most absolute kind. From the moment I cross your threshold I will have totally lost control of my life, your power will be supreme, such that I am your creature and you my goddess.

To that end I am open to whatever methods you and your friends have access to, so as to achieve this absolute power, whatever the source from which you derive it. The contract should include clauses that stipulate my acceptance. Should I disobey or dissatisfy you or your friends in any respect whatsoever, and in particular, should I attempt to leave before I am dismissed, whether by entreaty or open rebellion, you have the right to use whatever force you deem necessary to render me helpless, and thereafter to punish me as long and sadistically as you at your sole discretion deem appropriate. If you would endeavour not to leave any marks upon my body; but I understand that you could not guarantee this if you or your friends were forced to take emergency violent action to prevent my open rebelliousness or attempt to escape.

If in the contract you would make me accept methods of coerçion ranging from the physical to mind-control, employing hypnosis, psychic powers, light drugs (grass or Rush), magic ritual, extra-terrestrial energies, *et cetera.* By these extreme measures I should accept not only being your slave and prisoner but would become your creature, offspring of the goddess, a creature whose religion it is to worship you.

I know this is more than you have ever heard from me in our acquaintance. But I am ripe now for a major transformation. I hope it is you who reaps the benefit. But if you don't have time or interest, let it be a friend. I would be very grateful if it could be Mistress Katarina. But does she aspire to such a degree of control? No-one knows better than she how to crush me. I worship her body and soul. But the moment has come for me to be exposed to a woman with a will to absolute domination, with the psychological knowledge that tells her what methods and speeds will best achieve her goal. I think you have special psychic powers. Are you a witch? What do I mean by a witch? The ultimately Superior woman, who rightly uses her extra-natural powers to achieve noble objectives, in this case, your triumph over the male, to reduce him to his proper role of dedication to the worship of feminine glory.

Forgive the length of this but I hope it all serves to help you devise what I hope will be an irresistible strategy. In the meantime I enclose a check to compensate your time in reading this supplication, writing some reply, and drafting the contract of submission.

Your respectfully, D.

Terence Sellers

Dear Creature,

Your letter pleased and gratified Leila and I and we are ready to believe you when you say your desire is not only for your usual physical crushing but a true metaphysical submission. I have been in the past impressed with the little contracts you brought us and your obsession that you be forced 'beyond my control' – which sad to say you never achieved, at times growing so violently resistant it seemed not in our best interest to keep you at hand. I always did feel that you had a deep capacity for submission, and this letter proves it. You are fortunate that both Leila and I will be in town the week you arrive. I understood your panic, your need to rush away from me and regain your puny 'control' upon your life – you have manifested however real ability to completely lose your ego and be subsumed into that greater something than yourself, which you must know or suspect will free you in ways you do not yet comprehend.

The gratuity you enclosed and your sincere entreaties have made Mistress Leila and I consider for longer than a few minutes your request for a prolonged session. I hope you will actually appear and not disappoint us. I for one am bored by the pitiful one-hour submissions most slaves offer. I have been cultivating for the last few years, as befits my superior experience, a few select toys who can grant me that fuller satisfaction through a prolonged submission. I relish the breakdown that occurs under such extreme conditions. As much experience as you have had at our hands, it is as nothing compared to the Initiation you will know into an absolute submission and transformative loss of self.

I have determined that your ordeal will extend throughout the three days you have said you were available. The programme for those five encompassing days follows. The context for the session will be the Rite of Initiation into the 1st and 2nd degrees (of the 3 degrees) of Sex Magick, as detailed in a text that I will lend you prior to our commencing. To prepare yourself for this attainment, you must first of all make it very clear, in your mind, what you wish to achieve not only on the physical level but the psychic. Cleansing and purgation of your heart of useless worldly ambition might be part of your intent in this ecstatic practice.

Donald must submit to Dorian[1], so that the desirable egoless malleable state can be maintained.

When you read the text you will agree that in unconscious fashion we have already to a great extent achieved the first degree, Alphaism, and the second, Dianism. It is the third we are aiming for, but I do not hope to attempt Quodosh on our first try. This is the highest, orgasmic bliss wherein you are united with the Divinity. We have approached it, but not entered into it wholeheartedly. You are an excellent subject for this working as you hear every resonance and follow every gesture with an admirable attention. You understand the pathways we might cut, through flesh, into Spirit. To explain a bit further, the first degree, Alphaism, achieves a high sexual and psychic stimulation and maintains that level, without orgasm. This aspect we of course understand quite well. I quote from the text:

"Dianism may be practised for any purpose or desire and with success, providing that the intent conform with the conditions which any psychologist stipulate, i.e. that the objectives and desires be not in conflict with one's true nature."

Hence you may wish for anything in the course of the ritual, and we will focus our energies strictly to that end. It need not be anything relating to me, or to your sex-life or relationships, though it ought not be related to finance. No-one else involved need know of this end, which I would prefer to know so I might control and direct the proceedings in harmonious confluence.

My end is to further my control over another's body, mind and soul, to achieve the pleasure of maintaining that subjection for up to five days. I also wish to help you achieve your desire to not only lose yourself, but to be impressed with the imperatives of a Higher Power.

Programme For Dorian, September 16–20

Monday, 9/16. Upon arriving at your hotel you will telephone and inform us of your intent to undergo the Rites. You will have dispatched a messenger to advance us our required tribute, and to

---

[1] Donald: Slave Dorian's 'real' name.

pick up the Sex Magick text and other missives we may wish you to read prior to you appearance.

8pm. Plan to arrive at the Dungeon. You should have eaten well as you will not be fed until the next day in the late afternoon. Obeisance and first submission: all clothing, wallet, your passport, *et cetera*, will be surrendered; slavish dress such a collar will be assumed. Bring any garb you deem appropriate. Preparation of the body through anointing and some binding. Reinduction into the Mysteries of the Sanctum Sanctorum. Reading aloud of the contract and signing of the contract. Kneeling before the Altar to wait the arrival of all goddesses.

9pm–2am. Mistresses Leila, Katarina, Dominique, Pamela, Sonja, and Francoise in attendance. Ritual of the Purgation of Donald/Assumption of Dorian. Drinking of potions, infumations, to aid in achievement of trance. Severe bondage as a form of softening. Trials by Pressing, Enfolding and Crushing. Preparation of the flesh for the Sacrifice. Capture of the soul of Dorian. Trial by Trampling. Trial by Cocooning. Final bondage and Abandonment.

Tuesday, 9/17. Release from bondage, cleaning and shopping. The maid will give you my tray to bring in to me. No breakfast allowed. Discussion of the effects of the night's rituals. Return to bondage to await...

12 noon... arrival of Mistresses Venus, and Helena. I will leave you to their tender mercies.

3pm. You will be given some nourishment, and allowed a temporary reassumption of Donald, to make phone calls and attend to business.

4:30pm–8pm. We will be coming to the end of our first twenty-four hours. Trance-state will be maintained artificially if your attention has begun to lag. Depending upon your reaction you will be held in strict bondage, or not. Trial of inanimity; use as couch or mattress. Wrestling contest to be held with Mistresses you feel most submissive with. Attachment of locked bondage device upon

---

genitals. Dismissal to your hotel. Passport will remain with me to assure your appearance on 9/19.

Wednesday, 9/18. Dinner at 8pm with myself and Mistress Leila. Discussion of the next day's programme and its variations.

Thursday, 9/19. We will require you for the entire evening, through the night and morning. You will be dismissed at breakfast-time, 9/20. Details of this evening I do not wish to presently determine; much will depend on your response and reaction. You can depend on me to be artfully spontaneous.

I do not need to hear from you, Dorian, until you arrive in Manhattan. I am working on the contract, as well as a statement concerning what the strictures of your long-term submission would be. Your letter arrived here so late there is no time to arrange for or mail photographs, as per your request for further expository. I enclose one small picture of Mistress Leila to torment you for the stupidity of sending such an important missive by regular mail. I must add, too, that your letter's physical presentation was a disgrace, for which you failed to apologise. Scribbling, cross-outs, babyish 'high-lighting' as though we wouldn't be able to determine what was essential in your letter, and last of all a wretched stapling together of paragraphs that proved you were too lazy to rewrite it presentably. You are only forgiven because I was amused by your evident franticness. Your penmanship however will be tested and graded, so get to work on your cursive hand.

Yours in Elysium, Angel Stern

P.S. Please be assured that the ritual magick is enacted under the highest ethical standards, with no intention of a permanently harmful or deleterious 'draining' effect. You mental well-being is our first consideration, *after* we are apprised that dominating you will be *our* pleasure, which it shall be.

Dear Mistress Angel,

I know you said you did not need to hear from me until my arrival – but I had a long plane journey and I could not obey your demand, over the phone, that I do not excessively fantasize. I could not think of anything but you and what is to come. In mitigation I hope these pages will help you further know me. I eagerly await the reading of our Contract and hope you don't think I'm trying to script our relationship.

I enjoyed our conversation so much. You told me it is not so frequent that someone reaches the level at which I now am. To give you an idea of the magnitude of this for me, let me tell you I have never before revealed my real name to any Mistress; never have I placed in a Mistress' hands these secrets in writing; never have I offered to sign a contract, with my real signature; never have I laid myself open to occult power; never have I offered my passport as security. And last of all, I have never revealed my metaphysical yearnings for never have I met anyone who began to understand what you know so well. As for pot, yes – I was subjected to it – its use and its abuse – with a Mistress in London who has since gone back to Australia. I can vouch for the unusual effectiveness of pot, because without one ounce of your intelligence, that Mistress was able to achieve incredible breakthroughs in me with it.

Although I understand that you will release me Tuesday at 8pm, I have avoided all commitments for Tuesday evening, as I suspect when I go back to my hotel I will be longing for more, and more, and I beg you to consider taking me out to some sex-club and furthering my submission in ways I will not even try to imagine. I say to you "Anything" with all my soul!

This letter is not as neat as you would like, and the attached I admit is a mess as the airplane 'stationery' is as good as toilet paper and would not make erasures... I apologise... with greatest admiration and expectation... D.

Suggestions For The Contract

I. The Form Of The Contract

You will decide whether you prefer a contract in the sense of
A) that we are both of us parties to it, or
B) I make a Unilateral Declaration of total submission.

In the case of A, it would be in two sections, first a listing of everything I would agree to, and second, an outline of your demands, which hopefully would include those things I have wished for. In the case of B, the Unilateral Declaration, there would be a very long list of all my desires and undertakings, to end with a statement "the above undertakings are subject only to x, y, z" and there would follow a list of my limitations.

II. Amendments To The Contract

A. All that I have put in my previous letter to you and all that you have written to me can be attached to the main contract and marked as holding and binding.

B. I renounce any right to plead for changes in the contract after I have signed it; during its duration it overrules anything whatsoever I say.

C. I renounce all freedom to you in every respect during its duration.

D. I accept and even request the use of any force deemed necessary to hold me to the terms of the contract.

E. I declare that I accept all risks and understand the risk involved in undergoing this contract; whereas these obligations are limited to the contract period, that your powers may be so great as they may have a permanent effect and I accept that risk as well.

F. I accept that whereas these undertakings are made as a contract is transferable to any of your friends; I am your property and may be lent, sold, or traded, and that by definition whomever I am transferred to holds all rights accrued to you, Angel Stern, under the contract.
1) Whereas you will ask your friends to whom I am transferred to respect the limits of our contract, I accept the risk that they will not,

and I here renounce any notion of holding you responsible for the actions of others.

G. I accept the loss of my passport, wallet, and my name, and that they will not be redeemed until the termination of the contract.

H. I declare that the contract has been signed by me under no coercion whatsoever but that of my compulsive need to worship, for which I take fullest responsibility.

I. That I have the option of going out once on the morning of Tuesday, the 17th, to attend to some few business matters, such as phone calls and faxes. You could require me to be escorted so I might not escape.

J. That you will take care of my need to eat and relieve myself in a decent manner; but that I accept your right to give me no food at all.
1) I am anyway too fat.
2) Why trouble yourself to provide more than a biscuit.

III. Suggested Limits To The Contract

A. Unless otherwise suggested by me, drugs should not be imposed with the exception of pot, or a sleeping pill. I cannot tolerate alcohol either.

(One thing does worry me about pot. Given your enormous powers and the extreme suggestivity I am subject to under pot I worry if I will not get into one of those pathetic changes of mind when I really want to leave no matter what, and I start begging, then resisting, shouting and threatening. I do not want this to happen, but if it does, is it not tempting for you, having received the full tribute, to frankly throw me out after one hour? For me it is absolutely vital that you do not allow me to leave before the first twenty-four hours are up. In your letter you rightly criticise my failing to achieve being forced to stay beyond my control. But you did let me go! I realize that on these occasions I sound very convincing because I do mean it, but I see that I was creating a disturbance and you wanted to get rid of me. Gag me if necessary, and through the entire session. It is perhaps better for a high-powered intellectual such as myself to have no recourse in speaking, to persuade you. Shouting, I do admit is a cowardly act. Anyway, please put assurances in the contract that you will not allow me to leave, for however long it is determined, before the time is up. I cannot imagine that you would dismiss me, because of the long-term lucrative subservience you will receive from me if you keep me the full time, even if I hate you for it in the short-term.)

B. If it needs be that you must use force to restrain me you will do it in such a way as to leave no marks on my body. My skin marks very easily, and a severe whipping would last on my person for several weeks. Of course I could not be struck in the face. Given your great skills I am certain this will be no restraint upon you.

C. If in the course of the domination any men are present as slaves or Masters I would request that I am not asked to have any physical contact with them. I would also request nothing be inserted into me as it is so painful it only arouses unnecessary antibodies.

D. The contract is valid for the period of September 16-20, for approximately 36 hours altogether, and not beyond.

E. Confidentially.
1. The contract is a confidential document held between us. I trust you will not make copies of it or offer it for publication. You destroy it upon my departure. (Perhaps this is not necessary.)
2. I am paranoid about it "being known" that I have this compulsion to be dominated. You understand why. This paranoia means I am always covering my traces.
    I hope you understand what an enormous step it was for me to write you a check, and for that sum. I feel I can do it as you have too much integrity to sell any story about me to the press. Please assure me again that my judgement is correct.

F. 'Realism'
Many things drive me to you, although I understand few of them. One of them is them is the incredible sense of a surrender to real

power when you strangle me, smother me, squeeze my neck between your knees, *et cetera*. I know you are not acting, that you truly enjoy it. Those Mistresses who are your well-trained warrior women convey that feeling too – everyone seems to mean it – to be truly dominant – to embody my ideal. So often it's a paid artificial game that I ultimately control. I want the real me to be dominated by real women. What do I mean by 'real'? That you don't have to be dressed in leather or exotic outfits to hold me in thrall. That you can elicit from 'women unacquainted with true submissiveness' an interest in becoming dominant – that is real power! I admit I felt as though I were swooning when you said that, over the telephone, in your unbelievably seductive voice. Could these women participate, too – not just stand by as witnesses?

On the same 'realist' track, of the idea of participants, could you take me into a lesbian club? I know they have them in New York. I have no idea what lesbian women would think of the male slave, if they would get a kick out of it. Probably my presence would produce zero interest. This stimulates some strong fantasies in me. I could be used as an inanimate object, an ashtray, a stool, a doormat. I could be stripped naked by force, as if I were to be raped, outnumbered twenty or fifty to one. They could take turns slapping me around, from one end of the bar to the other. Maybe such things don't happen at lesbian clubs or are not permitted.

More on 'realism': can one mix domination and friendship? In our telephone conversations you sound very normal, you are cordial and you laugh. On the other hand when I spoke to Veronika on the phone, she sounded threatening. It's not a criticism of her, because she is fantastic, but the latent power in your normal, cordial voice was greater than the power in Veronika's threatening one. I can't really keep up with the outline form, I hope you forgive me, my thoughts are rushing all over, everything relates to you, you are in everything – I could write a treatise! I am convinced of your occult powers and anticipate being devastated, metaphysically; of having my ego taken from me; use these powers to their fullest extent, I beg you! Only one warning: I did have a Catholic upbringing and any reference to Satan himself would produce antibodies. Any other force, or goddess is fine. Let me offer one idea: concentrate on the possession of my soul for the duration of the contract. But I must add that the use of the 'forever' brings on a flurry of antibodies. It's a question of tactics, and you in the end will be the best judge, but it strikes me that if you do achieve this total metaphysical subjugation of the slave Dorian within the first twenty-four hours, without provoking too many antibodies, that 'forever' will follow naturally because I will be yours.

If you are expert in the use of hypnosis, I would submit to this, as it would increase my susceptibility to you. I think an entire separate contract would have to be drawn up however stipulating what suggestions I would be given and what I would not accept. I am sorry to make so many conditions – perhaps we'd better forget the hypnosis, this time!

I am a slave to feminine beauty and you are all beautiful. Far more effective than torture is the flaunting of your beauty. Caress me, excite me, seduce me, even make me feel I had the chance of making love to you. Then suddenly of course reject me utterly.

Maybe there is some music that can help you. I particularly like Wagner because his music is exceptionally enveloping. It takes me over. The Tristan and Isolde duet, when Tristan has taken the potion that obliges him to be in love with Isolde enraptures me. Or the awakening of the warrior goddess Brunhilde – or, above all, the Dance of the Valkyries, that wild and devastating sound. Should you play Wagner when you have me wrecked on pot and are working out the metaphysical subjugation, your task will be simple. I would like to produce an association between you and the music. Do you like Wagner? Tell me if you prefer CDs or tapes and I'll get everything for you. If we use Wagner, I will think of you every time I play it, and inevitably be driven to get on a plane and come to renew my servitude. The idea is that there would then be something I could play at home to trigger the compulsive thoughts, conjoined to the beautiful memories.

I admire your taking on the challenge of dominating a high-powered intellectual, your understanding how this metaphysical domination works upon me better than any command to vacuum. Subtlety is all... for that reason I particularly liked the idea in your letter about the morning ritual, serving your breakfast in bed and discussing the effects of the night's rituals. I think that interludes of deep discussion, including moments of precarious friendship, would be a great honour. Between bouts of domination we could discuss points of common interest – films, books, travel, criminology?

Concerning our long-term relationship, I do admit there are many things that tie me to the 'normal life'. I still must limit the sphere of domination to occasional and secret events. You said you would prepare a statement concerning my long-time submission. I await it with fascination.

My fantasies as to giving up my 'double life' vary. Perhaps I will only move into these prolonged, twenty-four to forty-eight hours ordeals. Or we could travel somewhere far away, where no-one would know me, and I could live as your valet, like Severin in *Venus In Furs*. My fantasy here prefers the greatest possible realism – a mixture of domination with friendship. I am realistic enough to know that I am still just a client, and that I ought not to presume that you would want to spend weeks with me. This brings us to the other fantasy: that I totally give up my 'double life'. I am wealthy enough to do so, to purchase a house and place it in your name, where I would be employed as your servant, under a pseudonym. I could tell friends and associates that I was writing a book and needed total isolation. I imagine what a year would be like under such conditions! It would have to be a Mistress who could remain as high and mighty as ever, while being somewhat dependent upon me financially (except for the ownership of the house, which would serve as the year's tribute). Then, I imagine that we are able to forgo and forget such things as contracts – that we are actually happy together, and decide to remain in the house at the year's end. I know this is an impossible dream, because there are so many things I would have to give up. But the dream itself inspires me, I feel I am moving towards something that most men would envy.

What appeals to me more than anything is what you called 'complete loss of ego', and the 'being subsumed into something greater than myself'. I know that the absolute certainty that I would not be dismissed for the extent of my visit would aid in that reduction of myself. I wonder if at least on this one occasion you would waive your right to use dismissal as a punishment?

I long to be absorbed into your divine totality. Am I right in believing in female superiority? I envisage that totality as being embodied in the Goddess-Made-Flesh. I beseech you to tell me if your occult arts are inspired by the Goddess, and not a confused, male Satan! They could not, you share my belief that the correct destiny for a man is to surrender to the Eternal Feminine! The world's best hope lies in this submission, which will only bring harmony, peace and beauty. But before that happy ending, centuries of male abuse must be expurgated and avenged by the female warriors. In that task of vengeance, it is my privilege to be an exemplary victim.

All my love, Dorian

September 16th
Manhattan

Dear Dorian,

We await your arrival this evening. Your enormous letter was perused; but you see the contract has already been drafted (enclosed). When you read it however you will discover that I had already wormed my way into your fevered brain. We will simply append your letter, with certain paragraphs struck out, to this document. We may discuss it a bit tonight, when you read it aloud, but I am not in the way of accepting a delay of your submission. We have received your tribute. Do not be late.

Mistress Angel Stern

CONTRACT concerning the SUBMISSION of dorian to his MISTRESS
ANGEL STERN

including elements relating both to transitory circumstance
and to submission in perpetuity

being a documents engendered by two consenting adults
for the .purposes herein described, to wit, that of
the slave dorian's yielding to the Domination of
the Mistress Angel Stern during the Hours of Control

From the _____ day of _____ at _____ o'clock
until the _____ day of _____ at _____ o'clock

the will of dorian is subject to, and shall be assumed into the Will
and Power of the Mistress. Due to certain weaknesses in the person
of dorian We have allowed for the following exceptions to his
perfect submission, these being his limitations, which shall stand as
immutable except as pertains under Section I-B-1 of the Contract:

1) No permanent or lasting marks of any kind will be inflicted upon
the body of the slave.
2) There shall be no enforced homosexuality or penetration of any
kind.
3) The slave will not be forced to take alcohol, cocaine or heroin.
4) The slave's true identity shall be made known to no-one, nor will
the Mistress break this trust and reveal the true nature of her
relationship with slave dorian to any person, for any reason.

Here follows Mistress Stern's conditions and requirements for the
perfect enslavement of dorian. Some sections do apply only for this
transitory phase, and will be replaced in the future with other
conditions. Other sections will pertain to dorian's submission in
perpetuity. Should they not be attainable at this time, they shall be
held in his mind as the quality of the submission he ought to attain
to.

I. THE PHYSICAL SUBMISSION

Terence Sellers

A. Slave dorian will not be allowed out of the control of the Mistress Angel or her associate Mistresses during the Hours of Control

    1. Manifestations of distrust – panicking, arguing, fighting, shouting, rejection, flight, or failing to return after the first twenty-four hours will be met with force and punished as severely as We deem appropriate.
    2. Any important business matters must be reserved for the time after the first twenty-four hours. Any crucial matter to be attended to must be conducted over the telephone, in Our presence, naked and kneeling.

B. Slave dorian is an owned piece of property, and as such may be subject to being sold or loaned to other Mistresses, with all advantages accruing to Mistress Angel passing unconditionally to the new permanent or temporary Owner.

    1. Should the new Owner(s) show no respect for the limitations of the slave, which shall be made known to Them, dorian will not hold Mistress Angel responsible for any ill-effects resulting from the violation of those limits.

C. Every submissive and/or masochist pleasure residing in the body of dorian will be exploited by the Mistress and suffered with delight by the willing slave.

    1. Slave will be mercilessly squashed, crushed, sat upon, rolled upon, wrestled, trampled, treated as furniture, held in bondage for unlimited periods, and rendered a prisoner who shall know no escape.
    2. He will experience his subjection to the powerful muscles of the Mistress with gratitude.

D. Slave dorian agrees to take into his body certain mild drugs to assure his Mistress of the maximum malleability of his body and mind.

E. Slave dorian will relinquish his passport and other important personal effects as a condition of his submission, to prevent in part his fleeing before the Hours of Control have passed.

1. dorian's passport will not be returned under any circumstance until the Hours of Control are passed
2. In the instance of severe disobedience, failure to return after the first twenty-four hours, or violent threats of an obnoxious nature by the slave dorian, his passport and personal effects will be mailed by slow boat to his home in London at 9pm, Friday, 9/20.

F. Slave dorian will be fed, allowed to wash and relieve himself, to experience sexual feelings, to move his limbs, and to speak only upon the express permission of the Mistress, which is granted subject to the whim of the Mistress.

G. Slave dorian will compensate the Mistress Angel Stern generously for the time spent in bringing him to ultimate submission.

1. Misbehaviour fines may be exacted in advance for potential errors in obedience.
2. Additional tributes will be exacted for extra time spent with additional Mistresses.
3. Though she receives a tribute for her time, Mistress Angel is not in service to dorian and may dismiss him at any time before the Hours of Control have passed, without his receiving any reimbursement. Being subject primarily to the Whim of the Mistress he is thus bound to be on his best behaviour.
4. If dorian forcibly escapes the Mistress before the Hours of Control have passed

a. he may not ask for, or expect a reimbursement.
b. an escape-fine of $3,000 will be exacted before the Mistress will consider undergoing his training again.

5. The setting of tributes, fines, and compensatory gifts follow no rule or schedule and are subject to infliction under the Whim of the Mistress.

II. THE EMOTIONAL SUBMISSION

A. Slave dorian will trust his Mistress unconditionally, and with a perfect kind of husband-like love will honour and obey her during the Hours of Control as well as In Perpetuity.

B. Slave dorian's propensity to panic and flee, to reject and distrust must be reflected upon by him while in bondage-isolation. He will confront the reason behind this behaviour, analyse it and make a thorough report to his Mistress Angel at the end of the Hours of Control.

III. THE PSYCHIC SUBMISSION

A. Slave dorian acknowledges the natural Superiority of the Dominant Woman, and agrees that he is an unevolved specimen before her.

B. Slave dorian renounces all freedom to think, act, or speak in any way that was not determined and approved by the Mistress in advance.

     1. Thought-control, and assumption of the proper attitude are disciplines to be explored in perpetuity.

C. The slave agrees that the Mistress is in possession of Superior Powers the nature of which he is not fully knowledgeable, and may never be conscious of; under their sway he will fall with gratitude and all humility.

D. The slave submits trustingly to every suggestion and command of the Mistress, putting his intellectual acuity in abeyance towards the end of benefitting his other less developed faculties, for example, his creativity, his own psychic abilities, his responsiveness and compassion for others, *et cetera*.

IV. THE INTELLECTUAL SUBMISSION

A. Once the slave dorian has agreed to the terms of the Contract, he may not change his mind, beg for changes, correct the Mistress or in any way try to alter the letter of the Contract, until the next full term of Control.

1. The Mistress may change any of the terms of this Contract at any time for any reason, short of usurping dorian's limitations.

B. Mistress Angel does not require dorian's total intellectual submission, as she considers his well-educated mind a treasure-box through which she may pick and choose for her private delectation. However he must never manifest any overweening superior attitude in thought or words, unless it should be specifically called for by her.

1. Should slave dorian note a lack of intellectual development in any Mistress-associate of Mistress Angel's, he will not condescend to her nor in any way make her feel inferior to him, for example, he will not correct their use of words. Nor will dorian think any less of such a Mistress, indeed he will strive to make himself appear stupid in her presence.
2. The slave dorian will endeavour to put his well-honed mental faculties to the purpose of true submission to Mistress Angel, and cease at once the exclusive consideration of his own self-aggrandizement.

a. The slave will attempt to place his intellect wholly at the disposal of Mistress Angel, in the case of her requiring from him scholarly drudge-work, towards the end of her literary work. dorian may be required to do research, look up references, purchase books, dropping all other pursuits to aid her in her endeavours.

C. The slave dorian accepts the reality that the influence of the Mistress Angel Stern will have a permanent effect on his life and ways of thinking, and he accepts in advance this overarching influence with all gratitude and humility

V. THE METAPHYSICAL SUBMISSION

The slave dorian understands well that he no longer has any choice but to undergo the transformative process of submission under the dictates of the Dominant Woman. He will become Nothing: this We achieve through an apparent inverse of the motions of evolution. First he will be shorn of his false male ego, reduced to the innocent trembling dependence of the child; then he will be rendered mute and weak as an infant; passing on to embryonic, unformed, utterly inert states; and then, at last, he will disappear. During the time that he is Nothing, when he has lost hold of himself as he once was, he will never be abandoned by the Mistress; indeed he will be totally protected. (He will be drawn out of this deepest submission, however, should it be decided that ownership will be transferred, lest some undue trauma occur.) The slave dorian will find himself passing in and out of this deepest submission, as in a fluid state. Towards the end of the Hours of Control he will be drawn out and rendered up to his old ego, worn polished for certain but enlivened, with a greater capacity for feeling and receptivity.

You will be killed, and die, slave dorian. *Liebestod is the essence of the submission that I, Angel Stern, desire.* I want you to know your most intense desire, express it completely, achieve and remain at that fever-pitch of your intention to please and gratify us, and merge with our Power. Though you will thus exalt yourself and become worthy of our notice, you will at the same time remain forever unsatisfied. To achieve one's aspirations only shows one the next pinnacle to climb. You will yearn to attain to a true intimacy, will desire us, need us, and come very close to Knowing Us. But do not believe that you will ever completely attain to your Ideal. This is as it should be. Be grateful that you are, at least, pointed in the correct direction.

I, slave dorian, aka D_____ Y_____, have read and fully accept the conditions of this Contract between myself and the Mistress Angel Stern, this _____ day of _____, 1990.

Signed, _____

[The following short note in Angel Stern's hand must suffice as the conclusive word on this contractual agreement. *Editor's note*]

[Dated 9/17]

After the 18th hour Dorian was reduced to a weeping, grovelling mass of mixed insult, imprecation and pleas. He crept into his sleeping box, curled up in the foetal position, sobbing most broken-heartedly. This was sparked by his hearing Mistress Venus say something to someone on the telephone about a video-camera. It had nothing to do with him but it set off the antibodies. During his paroxysm he begged me to allow him to call his girlfriend in London – I refused. He moaned and carried on, why was he doing this, he loved her, he loved his girlfriend more than anything in the world, why was he like this, why couldn't he be happy? *et cetera*. After being told he could not call this woman, he rushed to my desk to grab the 'phone and had to be restrained. He fell asleep sobbing in his sleeping-box in light bondage. He slept until one hour was left in the first twenty-four; then a sincere, confiding conversation apprised us of the impossibility of his going through with the entire programme. We enjoined him to do so, despite appearances.

9/19. Dorian arrived on time, but only to cancel. We gave him back his passport. He whined that we had not called him at his hotel to demand his return! We did not deign to respond to this, especially as his pettish cancelling precluded any further involvement from us. Erratic, changeable, unstable, inconsistent. When asked why he hadn't called yesterday to cancel the dinner-date, he gave no satisfactory answer. For the future we must limit extended sessions to twenty-four hours, if that. $3,000 reinstatement fee waived.

the doctor-mistress of brian g. and her medical papers

The case of Brian G. advances a serious warning to those slaves whose tastes tend to the severer punishments. Though his story had a somewhat happy ending, we fear the average injured client will not meet with the same enlightened treatment Brian fortunately enjoyed.

Eight years before our meeting, young Brian arrived in Manhattan from England, and quickly set about trying to find the fabled Dominatrix who might gratify his budding desire for erotic punishment. He happened upon an inexpensive establishment, where were employed women of a quality not strictly Dominant. Brian chose a young lady, requested bondage, and then, naively, enjoined her to play upon his body in whatever way she preferred. This person thereupon forced an unlubricated instrument into his anus – which operation was horrible enough – but the object itself was cracked, and a hard, plastic edge cruelly lacerated the lining of his rectum. As blood poured forth in profuse quantity, the 'lady' in question *left the premises* – abandoning Brian, still in bondage, to bleed to death. Nor did anyone answer his cries for help. Fortunately her amateur knots enabled him to untie himself and escape, wadded with towels, to the nearest emergency room.

This experience might have rendered Brian traumatized and frustrated for the rest of his life, had not the Doctor in charge of his case been a lady of great skill – as well as possessed of a highly-developed sadistic inclination. She cared for Brian's injuries in excellent fashion, and some days afterwards conferred with him in confidential manner. She revealed her understanding of what he had been trying to accomplish sexually, and invited him to consider an Initiation into practices and pleasures of which he had yet but the slightest inkling. Brian agreed, and the horror-story that evening might have been resolved itself into a seven-year relationship.

During·that time Brian was taught everything that his body was capable of withstanding. Under her strict and accomplished methods, she developed his taste for torment to a refined degree. After his seven years in training, sadly for Brian, his Doctor-Mistress discovered her true-love Doctor-Slave, married, and left the Manhattan area. We received his case-history with the greatest interest, especially as Brian informed us of the existence of a subculture of Doctors, Nurses, and other medical professionals all of whom are deeply involved in the sexual aspects of pain and imposed torment, and the pleasures to be gathered therefrom. One may imagine how they might bring to the arts of S&M a wealth of knowledge of physiology, as well as surgical techniques – not to mention the deployment of catheters and enema-nozzles – that the average Master or Mistress garners somewhat haphazardly. We do observe that the need for a certain temperamental sadism would be useful in the medical profession. We may posit that to perform excruciant dental surgery, to cut bones, eviscerate, sew skin, impose traction, or to amputate demands a cool ability to impose pain. To be unfazed by screams and mildly indifferent to the flow of blood would be, admittedly, talents in that field. It was not so long ago that hearty types such as butchers and executioners were allocated the function of surgeon. Modern medical sadism will of course remain firmly subsumed in the service of the healing process, as a necessary and unselfish tool. But in the Doctor-Mistress we may note a re-emergence of the pride and pleasure in an efficient use of pain for pain's sake.

She who undertook Brian's rigorous education left behind her the following two esoteric papers concerning findings in the delicate practice of erotic penis-torture. This information I not only used with Brian, but later incorporated into other sessions, to good issue. I might here note that Brian G. was seen by us but a few times before he disappeared. We do not wonder that he was not much

Terence Sellers

gratified by our attentions, after the extravagantly skilled handling he had been accustomed to.

A Medical Paper On B&D Punishment,
By Anonymous

Although the author of this paper is a practising medical doctor, the terms 'Cock' and 'Balls' will for the most part be used for ease of communication and ideas.

The primary purpose of this paper is to discuss the heavy punishment (i.e: use of whips – specifically the so-called 'Cat-Of-Nine') of the male cock and balls.

In the interests of medical safety a description of the male sexual organs is necessary. The penis is the male copulatory organ through which the sperm duct passes. Its basic structure consists of three roughly cylindrical masses of spongy erectile tissue, with a loose outer covering of skin. Two of the cylindrical bodies, the *corpora cavernosa(s)* lay side by side; the third body, the *corpus spongiosum* is bulb shaped near the point of attachment of the penis to the pubic arch, narrows throughout the shaft of the penis, and widens greatly to form the head and tip of the penis, also known as the glans penis. Erection of the penis occurs when nervous stimuli trigger an increase in the supply of arterial blood to the erectile tissue; as the tissue swells it constricts the veins making the penis erect. Continued mental and physical stimuli keep the penis erect, the period of erection varying greatly with the individual; usually between a few minutes to several hours.

The ability of any penis regardless of size to receive punishment in the form of whipping varies according to many factors; including threshold of pain level, size including length and thickness and musculature structure and strength. Generally speaking the larger penis is able to withstand considerably more punishment than smaller penis.

From a medical point of view, whipping of the cock should be done in a standing position, with restrictive arm and leg bondage; this is especially true of heavy whipping. Additionally whipping should be varied with several light lashes, medium and heavy lashes; once a cock has been whipped for a few minutes the lashing

Terence Sellers

can be increased in harshness accordingly. It is also important that a cock ring be placed around and behind the sac of the balls during cock-whipping; said ring should be restrictive, but not totally by any means. With individuals used to receiving large amounts of heavy whip lashes (i.e: 100 plus in any given two hour period) marking of the outer skin will occur. This is not a medical problem as long as once the entire cock outer skin has been marked, whipping must be stopped, or remain very restrictive.

In regards to the balls (testicles), here we are dealing with a very sensitive part of the male body; which does not mean that the balls cannot be whipped. They can and should. As with the cock-size, musculature structure and strength dictate the heaviness of the whipping which can be given. However, heavy prolonged whipping of the balls must be undertaken with great care, as the testicles go through certain cycles, which if whipped heavily at the wrong time can cause problems. The sign of such cycles is an overall soreness of the testicles to hand massage; if such is present, only light to medium whipping 'that day' should be undertaken. This is not so much a problem with those individuals used to a regular heavy whipping of the balls (i.e: 100 lashes per session per week), as the body will automatically increase the depth of tissue and musculature structure and strength, in order to handle the regular heavy whipping punishment. It is vital though, that such individuals continue on a weekly or bi-weekly basis such punishment, as the body will reverse the process; and as such a heavy whipping (prolonged – i.e: 100 lashes or over) would be potentially medically damaging. Hence an extreme level of trust must be developed between the Mistress and the Submissive.

As to the harshness of whipping, lashes to the cock of light strength up to almost the severest one-armed lash (that the average built woman can give) are medically acceptable. In regards to the balls, the harshness can be from light to that of around two-thirds to three-quarters of the harshest lashes the individual's cock can take. Heavy whipping of the balls like the cock will cause swelling, which is to be expected. Whipping of the balls should cease when the outer skin is completely marked.

This concludes this private paper, which for reasons of confidentiality is not being signed.

A Specific Individual's B&D Capability,
By Anonymous

This note is being issued as an addition to the *A Medical Paper On B&D Punishment,* and concerns a specific individual the author saw on a regular basis as a submissive.

The individual in question is _____ who is originally from Britain, and has been involved in the B&D scene for many years.

This individual fits the description of someone who is able, from both a medical point of view and pain threshold perspective, receive an especially harsh punishment of both his cock and balls.

As to this individual's ability to take harsh cock-whipping, he is able to take between 100 and 200 heavy whip lashes per hour. In fact in a prolonged session I have whipped this individual's cock for over six hours (including other punishments as well), resulting in 1400 lashes to his cock. He is almost certainly capable of receiving 2000 lashes over an eight hour prolong session – this on the basis of a few hundred lashes per hour with other punishments in between.

Based on my experience, I can only recommend a 'Cat-Of-Nine' whip for all cock- and ball-whipping.

In regards to whipping of his balls he is capable of taking between 100 and 200 heavy whip lashes per two hour session, in groups of 50 to 100 lashes. Medically it is always better to give heavy ball-whipping in groups of 50 to 100 lashes at any one time during a session. I have in the same prolonged session noted above, whipped his balls with 700 lashes over six hours. It is likely he can take up to between 900 and 1000 lashes over eight hours.

A note on ball-whipping from a safe medical perspective. Except for light ball-whipping which can be done in a standing position in restrictive bondage, heavy ball-whipping must be done with the person in a laying position (table/bed, etc.) in extremely restrictive arm and leg bondage (mouth gag if they request), with the legs slightly elevated and wide apart. There should be a cock ring just behind the balls (not too loose or restrictive – seek submissive's help on this point), like whipping done from a standing position. Too restrictive bondage during heavy ball- whipping *will* cause medical damage.

Note: If any submissive has not had heavy cock- or ball-whipping in over three to four months, a period of two sessions to bring the submissive up to maximum ability will be needed. Question a submissive on this closely before initiating a heavy whipping.

This concludes this special note.

masochism in the service of the trivial modern man

"Men are unhappy because they have lost... the happy feeling of a rhythmic alternation between pleasure and pain."

We are familiar by now with the client who seeks to alleviate his real or imagined guilt through masochistic practices... with the fetishist who is unable to know pleasure except through fanciful submission... these forms of subjection having in common a psychic necessity which justifies their vulgar, hideous or crazed elements, granting them a private logic and orderliness. However it does happen that the infliction of pain is requested for utterly trivial reasons, that the cathartic release may be required for no extra-physical reason at all. The power of the Mistress-Master is thus manipulated towards a purely idle purpose – as spectacle, or in the service of inanity.

The Average Slave is of means, white and urban, with no actual pain in his life. No serious struggle for survival, no actual experience of violence, and often no real passion invests his paltry crawl upon the planet. Well-fed and generally content with the status quo, still there 'evolves' within his cossetted cells the need to know real suffering. Also, he is degraded by the peculiarly modern malaise of being passively entertained to the very brink of thought. Because he may remain indefinitely insulated in a warren of an apartment, or in the cosy nest of suburbia watching television, videos, sex-videos, playing with computerized 'interactive' games of war and sex, or logging onto the 'Internet' to hobnob with a seemingly infinite number of fantasy-psyches – is it imperative for him to ever again have an actual flesh-on-flesh experience, violent or joyful? It is all too easy to avoid the experience of true, individualised suffering, imposed by the uncontrollable unknown of another human. hand. The Mistress-Master's extreme, enlivening inflictions grant that dirty (if stylized) edge to the numbed psyche. Ideas of thrilling torment *would* become ideal to the isolated toy of technology that modern man is.

Even as the privileged one looks on with faint pity and disgust at the poor man's grim scrabble to survive, we know he at times craves that very insecurity. And so may the beggars laugh, derisive at those who would *pay money* in order to suffer. After the experience of deprivation, the client finds renewed again his pleasures in privilege. Only now, must the pain be evoked, with some regularity, to interrupt the flat monotone of satiation? Through the Master-Mistress he is denied gratification, disciplined, crushed under the harshest standards, reviled for his over-civilised, weakling, over-fed life. These hardships, though invented, may be for the sufferer psychically real. However, the Superior finds their fantasy of what constitutes torment truly laughable and wretchedly trivial when compared to what true masochists and ingrained perverts must, and will, endure.

Dialogue With A Trivial Modern Slave: 'Force Me To Lose Weight'

The Mistress is Head Nurse and the Slave is the Patient in the Doctor's examination room.

Nurse: Get on the scale!

Patient meekly steps up on the scale, causing it to creak.

Nurse: Two hundred and twenty-nine pounds! Tsk.
Patient: You oughtn't make comments about people like that.
Nurse: I don't recall that I said anything about your gross and monstrous shape.

Patient cringes as he is quite naked.

Nurse: And besides, why 'oughtn't' I? We are not here to protect that mess of blubber... we are here to destroy it!
Patient: But the Doctor says...
Nurse: The Doctor is not here today, is he? *I* am to record your efforts to remain on the diet *we* have set you!
Patient: But...
Nurse: We see from the chart that you have gained three pounds in the last four days. Did you eat meat every day? Did you drink sugary soda-pop? Did you gorge yourself on cakes? Did you indulge in chocolate candy? Did you drink beer? Have you stopped eating bread, potato-chips, and butter?
Patient: Yes... yes... no... I can't help myself.
Nurse: We can see that. Alright then – did you exercise? Did you do the sit-ups assigned to you? Did you take an aerobics class? Did you even go for a walk?
Patient: I didn't have time.
Nurse: You are a very, very sick man. You must truly hate yourself.
Patient: No! I love myself!
Nurse: But why? You love your fat? You love looking like a monstrous pig? You love inspiring disgust wherever you go?
Patient: Force me to lose weight.

Nurse: I don't know if it's possible. You have a pig-like nature, too content and grunting. We see you have a large and gaping maw, well-suited to the senseless shovelling into it of great piles of food. Now, I would like to know how you spent your time other than eating and sleeping, and devouring everything in sight, like an unevolved mollusc, like a great sleepy amoeba?

Patient: I watched television.

Nurse: Shouldn't you be out looking for a second job?

Patient: I am planning to.

Nurse: You are just another slave in this race of modern slaves. You are a stupid, blind animal of your senses.

Patient: You are right. I am a hog. If you could make me have more ambition, help me be more motivated...

Nurse: You would probably only make more money, to buy more food, so as to grow fatter and fatter and more content before a bigger, more expensive television set with remote control.

Patient: Give me something to do, mould me into something better – maybe I could work for you here, cleaning the office.

Nurse: Well, perhaps the Doctor might approve your being shipped to our Fat Ranch out West. We are always in need of new cattle.

Patient: I don't want to be a cow!

Nurse: Cow, hog, what's the difference? That's what you are, unless we can evolve you. Perhaps after spending a little time at Rancho Fatso, you can move up to being a Pony. And if your appearance continues to improve, you might even be promoted to Ranch Hand.

Patient: How long will it take before I can be a Ranch Hand?

Nurse: You might never get to be a Ranch Hand. You'll probably never even make it to Pony. Ponies are sleek and feisty, and get to give the nurses rides across the lonesome prairie. However, we might find a place for you at the new Zoo we're opening up for the impossible cases. How would you like to be a Hippopotamus Ride?

Patient: You'll see! I won't eat a thing, as long as you're there to discipline me. I'll lose all the weight and be your Ranch Hand.

Nurse: It's too much hard work. You'll never make it.
Patient: But aren't the Ranch Hands allowed to service the Queen of the Ranch?
Nurse: It can happen... but rarely.

Another famous case of a trivial slave was the golfer who came in dressed for the course, dragging his bag of golf-clubs with him. He had been practising all day and was set to be in a tournament, and requested Mistress Angel to tie him down, beat him and verbally abuse him. The theme of the punishment was, "You are going to win the tournament... you are going to par under sixty."

Pain was inflicted to the point of his screaming that he swore he would win – under pain of worse *tournoiements* would he play a perfect game.

By far the worse abuse of the Mistress' good faith occurred on an afternoon, with a little non-descript man who appeared in the Dungeon, carrying a brown paper bag. He requested Mistress Angel wear very high-heeled shoes, with sharp spikes, and trample the dead bird that he had in the bag. Though it seemed a nauseating enterprise, Mistress Angel agreed, assuming that in the scenario he had devised, of her being a cruel Aunt killing his pet, some unhappy unresolved trauma was at play. Though she insisted the poor corpse be placed between paper towels, as she crushed its bones its blood seep did out and soil her shoe. Never had she felt herself to be so completely a pervert as at that moment. As the man whimpered, "No, no, don't hurt the bird," and achieved orgasm, she rushed from the room to bathe her face in water, trying to reassume her Superior aplomb. As she came back into Dungeon, and saw the remains of the bird neatly thrown in the trash, she tried to divine from her client what was the basis of his fantasy.

"Did your Aunt kill your pet bird... when you were a boy?" she hazarded delicately.

Flatly he regarded her, "Aw... naw. I just found it on the street... on the way over. Thought it might be a good idea..."

So her act of desecration had been for his mere idle amusement. Because of the man's inanity, Mistress Angel felt, for years, that this act was the worst thing she had ever done. She was not really relieved to hear, some ten years later, of a slave who was making the rounds with a packet of goldfish, hoping to have them destroyed before his blank and avid gaze.

the fantasies of trauma: war-criminals and their victims

When Mistress Angel Stern began her practice in the late 1970s the American war in Vietnam had been over for three years. Certain of her clients were veterans of that war, and displayed a set of submissive fantasies and fetishes particular to that traumatic conflict. Among the forms of masochism to be observed were: fantasy of being a conquered 'coolie'; fantasy of the power of the military uniform, to wit being stripped of it; fantasy of weaponry and guns, of guns being used to force sex from them; fantasy of terror, of being placed in some extreme physical danger, of mutilation and castration at the hands of the enemy; fantasy of being killed, of looking one's killer in the eye the instant before death.

On the near-equal and opposite side, we might review certain sadistic fantasies prevalent certainly in war-time: fantasy of being served like a conquering hero; fantasy of the military uniform as a talisman of power; fantasy of the absolute power of weaponry, of using guns to force sex from others; fantasy of creating terror, holding people hostage, putting others in extreme physical danger, of mutilating the bodies of the enemy; the fantasy of murdering, of being a powerful killer, having the power of life and death over others.

But for this last, all these fantasies might be indulged in through a proper psychodrama. Though none of the ideas are beautiful, they might to good issue be sexualized and detonated in the explosion of orgasm. The turn of possible fantasy into probable reality stops at the strict black line separating we happy libertines from the Death-fetishist psychopath. While some few have experienced orgasm at the sight of one's dead handiwork, this disgusting behaviour is not in the Mistress' precinct. Yet it behooves the Superior to manifest no squeamishness when faced with any of the other fantasies, even though all have the dominating presence of death active in them as a third party.

We might consider these forms of masochism as reflective of the humiliating conception that the war had been failure – had been lost. Not only has the military, within itself admitted to the defeat, but the indifferent public at large looks upon these soldiers as somewhat less than noble. Indeed, were they not dupes of an authoritarian conglomerate that used them and most likely lied to them about the worth of the battle? These soldiers came home to public humiliation of enormous variety, which horribly increased the psychic pain, in many, of humiliations gone through only recently at the hands of the enemy. For these there was no succour – seemed to be *no reason* – for their having suffered and almost died. When castration like this is effected upon the warrior-nature of a man or woman, the damage is nearly irreparable. The left-over human being is not only incapable of reneging upon his commitment to soldiery: with pride destroyed they will never be able to see themselves nor love themselves as the powerful beings they once were. One group returning to a West Coast airport was forced to walk an infamous 'gauntlet of spittle' as they left customs; the images of glory most had treasured defaced forever in the slavering disgust of that radical leftist crowd. Verbal abuse was followed by contemptuous indifference; bureaucratic neglect not only of their physical ailments, but of their psychiatric problems created in many a fertile soil for the masochistic abreaction to ferment.

While some veterans of that war went on to kill themselves, or go on rampages with their beloved talismanic weaponry, others held within themselves silently, ominously, the accumulating humiliations.

Case of David #126: fetishist for women in military uniform. The Mistresses must wear as much leather as possible, pants or a long skirt preferred; brass buttons, false militaristic regalia such as epaulettes, mirrored aviator sunglasses, visored hat pulled down so only the severe line of the mouth is seen. He is verbally castrated as he worships boots, offers his face avidly for the most violent slaps. David spends much time on the telephone discussing the myriad possibilities of his crushing by militaristic female domination. Could we please wear Dr. Marten's instead of high-heeled patent-leather? When we slapped him with our black leather gloves on, would we please not take off the gloves, ever, in front of him? Could we find him a Mistress who had actually been in the WACs or WAVs? Didn't we think the nature of her violence would be more acutely cruel than ours? When he did show up for his sessions they were brief and violent – a warning had been appended to his card, to gag him as he approached orgasm.

Even so he could work the gag out, in order to be able to scream at the top of his lungs: "GODDESS... YOU FUCKING GODDESS!" this invocation echoing from basement to attic of the building.

Mistress Juliette once limped out of his session and we gasped in astonishment to see the crescent-shaped rip his orgasmic teeth had torn in the toe of her cowhide Dr. Marten's. Afterwards he would hang around endlessly talking to us, morosely describing his solitary existence, his longing for a girlfriend, philosophising about suicide, and analysing the effects of the latest psychoactive drug his latest psychiatrist had given him.

"Mistress, if I bring in a gun – will you hold it to my head?"

"Sorry David – no."

Case of William #153, client of sixteen years: large powerful body from the waist up, semi-atrophy of legs from war-injuries, must walk with a cane for his limp. First meeting was when the Mistress was called into a room in the establishment where she then worked, as the 'final solution' to a problem six girls were having with him. William lay naked face down, laughing and almost jeering at the 'ladies' who had exhausted their arms belabouring his buttocks and back. Blood flowed freely from hundreds of cross-cuts, as William smiled benignly upon Mistress Angel, and indicated there were still a few of the long thin rattan canes he favoured left unbroken. He received her blows with shining eyes and high approval, becoming her faithful client from that day.

As over the years his condition remained unchanged, Mistress Angel understood there was something in William that needed to be broken, and that it would be close to impossible for him to attain that release. At times the Mistress would think she heard a faint whimper, but, more often, in the midst of a violent attack he would observe, dissociatively, that the movie everyone was talking about was really quite the bore; that the woodwork in the room was really very fine – how old did we think the building was? A fine old building, really. We wondered where his limit for pain might be, if there was any – and what combination of pain, violence, abuse and understanding would bring him back into his deadened body.

One afternoon William seemed more than usually nervous and talkative. For some reason his capacity was shallower than the Mistress had ever known before. Within twenty minutes his ability to withstand pain without reaction had been reached. We determined to go on however, through the hour as usual. As his experience of sensitivity grew overwhelming, as he was able to feel everything that was done to him, he began to masturbate (which he did not often do, sometimes subject to spontaneous emission in the throes of the beating). I realized then my goal was to hear that whimper loud and clear.

From him a monologue began to pour forth: "I will not cry out... all my men are here, all my men are here. I will not cry out, I will not cry..."

So I continued in my violence, not relenting in the least.

Then a mantra emerged, "We're all together here, we're all together and naked; if I cry out we will all die. We're all together naked – my men are staring at me. If I cry out we will all be killed. I will not cry out, we will all be killed... naked... killed... together."

The tension was unbearable, but I knew that William was going deeper than he ever had before. Even his skin no longer evidenced that morbid hardness that made the blows bounce off him. I kept on, outside my own will, determined to bring him to a catharsis that had been years in its evolution.

To slash a bloody cane into a freely bleeding open wound is not exactly the most aesthetic of experiences, and as we reached the end of the hour I searched in vain for a clean spot to further berate.

He went on muttering ecstatically, "The men are watching... all the men are watching... they can kill me, I won't cry" as I struck him what I hoped was one last blow. A deep intake of breath – and William whimpered!

I screamed then "Coward!" to help him achieve orgasm.

In the grateful wash of his relief William explained to me the meaning of his words, and it was then I learned the full story of his P.O.W. experience.

His particular war-trauma had involved daily public whipping while a prisoner of war. His entire outfit had been captured, and he had been the highest ranking officer among the Americans in the torture-camp. The Vietcong kept them tied in a yard and beat them with impunity, for the sadistic fun some can enjoy upon unwilling subjects. As the ranking officer, it was desperately incumbent upon William to never show that he was the least affected by the blows.

The only way for the captives to bear the unspeakable violence being done to them was to show each other an unbroken will to conquer, demonstrating an absolute bravery and an unflinching strength. They would *not* bow before their conquerors, *not* submit to avoid further violence. The men looked up to William to lead the way – if he broke down, they might all.

William thus made himself into a shaman, his dominating will helping and shielding his tribe from loss of face – even at the cost of his bodily integrity. As he cared for his men, so he became their martyr; and martyr too to his country. He would embody the indomitable spirit of America! In the service of this Ideal was demanded from him an extraordinary effort, which he was quite capable of. His trial left him marked and crippled. Through psychodrama is again demonstrated the ability of the sexuality to absorb intolerable humiliation, and mercifully translate it into pleasure.

While William sometimes seems depressed, in general he is a kind and rather passive sort. He is almost courtly in his manners and manifests to every Mistress the greatest respect and gentleness.

Case of Nick, transient client: was completely open about his experience as a P.O.W. torture-victim 'at the Hanoi Hilton' – a euphemism used by the *cognoscenti* as code for torture upon the genitals, apparently a favourite sport of the Vietcong. Nick needed to be tied down so there was not the slightest possibility for movement. He then desired the Mistress to slash at his scrotal sac and penis with a razor-blade. As the operation began, he kept an eye on her procedure, commenting in a detached manner on the Mistress' methods.

From time to time he would gently admonish her, "That's not enough."

Before long of course it was time to desist, and he mildly complained, "It's never enough... it can never be the way it was before."

Minimal erection throughout the operation, a certain melancholy prevailing, and no orgasm. Why could he not achieve that level of pain he so desired? We assured him the next step would be permanent mutilation – but he was blasé. Was this strange nostalgia for an original horror only a kind of irony? He had taken as his profession after the war that of anaesthesiologist; but the removal of pain no longer granted him a resolving satisfaction.

Case of Hilda (Harry), client for one year: originally appealed to Mistress Angel to 'make him a total woman'. He arrived with an enormous wardrobe of ladies' lingerie, petticoats, dresses, wig and shoes – but no make-up. Upon his undressing the Mistress noted that Hilda was already dressed in more than one pair of tight nylon underpants and support-style pantyhose. During the period of this training not once did the Mistress view Hilda's genitalia. He was comical in drag, being of enormous height and breadth, with an imposing physique unsuited to pink. He too had been a P.O.W. at the 'Hanoi Hilton'; once told Mistress Pamela that he had known some soldiers who had been fully castrated there. Our 'Hilda' remained adamantly male, manifesting no effeminate traits, speaking always in his low male voice. She was a good tough houseworker and could reach into the high corners of the dungeon to sweep the cobwebs down. Expressions of sexuality during these sessions were never seen; she simply wished to perform her role well, and accepted being called 'Hilda' with a wan smile.

Case of Frank, transient client: subject apprised us of his desire to serve as a slave-'coolie', to do menial tasks and run errands. If he performed well, we would allow him to masturbate as a reward. He was sent to do the laundry, to go out and buy cigarettes, was sent back to the store because he bought the wrong cigarettes, then sent out again to fetch ice-cream.

During these mild torments Frank had occasion to view the condition of one of our favourite clients. 'Maryanne' was a sixty-ish, retired gentleman whose fantasy was that he might be a baby girl. Attired in a pink ruffled dress, diapers, and Maryjane shoes, Maryanne strutted up and down the corridor in the apartment, declaring in her loud, whiny voice that she would *not* be spanked, she would *not*. Frank looked at this apparition in a kind of daze, and once muttered, "I'm not into that."

No-one had suggested that he was, and, ignoring this warning, I, Mistress Angel, went on with the discipline of the brat, while Frank was left to the attentions of Mistress Susan, a young and somewhat inexperienced Mistress.

After 'Maryanne' had packed her bags and gone (and no doubt Frank had awaited her departure) I heard screams of rage emanating from the office. As I stormed in to investigate, Frank turned from a cornered Susan to accuse me, "You think I'm like that fucking perv, too, don't you? You think I'm a no-ball freak too!"

When I politely inquired how he wished to finish his submissive session, and informed him that we were *not* interested in his sadistic fantasies, he retaliated, "That's too fucking bad – whore! – because now you bitches are going to do what *I* say."

By his body language we could discern that he was dying to get into a physical brawl. I pretended to accuse Susan of mishandling him, knowing there had probably been nothing that could have prevented this outburst. Still he was not appeased, "You think you can get me to wear a dress, don't you, you were both planning on it, well fuck you I'm a man, a man, something sick whores like you don't know a thing about!"

"I was trying to give him his 'reward'... when he heard Maryanne leave he zipped up his pants and started this," Susan whined.

At this salient point he thrust his face into mine and screamed, "Do you understand that I'm capable of killing you?"

Then, to cap off this pedigree, he let us know he had been in Vietnam, he was a professional killer, and it would be as nothing to kill a couple of stupid whores who didn't know a real man from the hole he was going to put in their heads.

As over and over he raged, "You think I have no balls – you think I have no balls!" I compassionately gathered, given my knowledge of the delicacies offered at the 'Hanoi Hilton' that this might be precisely his case. As his illicit sadism waxed gloatingly triumphant – he had us trapped in our office, any attempt to move him towards the door, as we insisted that he leave, please leave, only increasing his frenzy – Mistress Angel knew instinctively the only solution was to assume the corresponding submissive role to his venomous domination.

As if she had suddenly been convinced of the truth of all he said, she began to agree with him. She was just a whore – a sick person who had never before in her life met such a real man. She asked him for a date, and 'suffered' his rejection. She admitted they had made a huge mistake in accepting him as a submissive client, that they should have known instantly he was a cut above the rest. She regretted his having seen Miss Maryanne in her glory – the sight of that older man reduced to the highest of feminine absurdity had triggered Frank's frenzy, terrorized him as a kind of *prediction* – of just what could happen to a 'no-ball freak'.

Psychiatric attitude had little effect. When he announced yet again he could kill us, I quietly said, "That must be very difficult for you to deal with."

"No, bitch, it's very difficult for YOU to deal with!"

After over an hour of high volume, continuously peaking hysteria, Frank moved to the door and began his vituperative good-byes, repeating the list of our imagined faults. Then, for no apparent reason, he was gone. In our subsequent prostration and nervous fits – especially in myself, who later vomited from the stress of submitting – we were not spared more of his reign of terror. He called on the 'phone about an hour later, "I'll be back, whores –

your killer will be back."

Happily he was never heard from again.

Transient cases: the day of the first air-strike of the U.S. on Iraq there were no telephone calls, no business at all, as the impending outbreak of war kept all preoccupied before the television... As superior American air-power began to decimate Iraq, a few appointments were made. As an hour, two hours passed and the triumphant attack went on – as it became obvious to all we were gloriously 'conquering' – the 'phone began to ring off the hook. All throughout that late afternoon and evening and into the night clients came clamouring for their punishment. This would be nothing to remark upon – mere release of a mass tension would be enough to account for it – except that more than half the clients requested military uniforms on the Mistresses, and insisted upon playing as captives of war: bound, humiliated, subject to our whim, tortured and beaten and interrogated for military secrets. It was touching – almost tragic – to see a group of older American men, not on the front lines of the current conflict – suffering the trials of the enemy side symbolically, and in simultaneity. While the rest of the culture did the dance of death, they instantly took on the guilt for the bombing, doing expiation for our war-crimes upon their own bodies.

why does perversion exist? cried the slave to his mistress

In the throes of his anguished orgasm, little Peter cries out to his Mistress, "Why am I doing this? Why can't I stop? Why – why does Perversion exist?"

Dear Peter, you would have your Apple and a Paradise too. You Know too much now – Know Yourself too well to go back to Innocence again. If ever you were – if Innocence is not a fantasy like all the others!

As the 'Sexual Revolution' broke in the 1960's, a tremendous power was unleashed in Western human consciousness. Women-on-the-Pill, freed from the hitherto necessary connection between sex-life and child-birth, were the agents for the loosening of the collective libido. Profanation of the sacrament of Venus (betrayal of the Service to Love that sex must be) became a commonplace, as Free Love was cried in the streets. But it was neither Love, nor Free, but a constant, gross expression of every permutation in sexual possibility, bringing in train their curses: endemic divorce, new diseases of Venus, rampant sex-crime, sexual dysfunction. Ah, the malignant varieties! In the volcanic wake, many know their sex not strengthened, but truncated, mutilated, killed off. To date millions have died in the great Mass Indulgence – many more than have come to true Liberation. For in the heady madness of untrammelled pleasure, one thought was not much spoken: that with Freedom comes acute Responsibility. By our culture's insistent ignorance of sex and the sexual instrument, the paradisal promise was too soon destroyed. So we are now beset with the ranting of Xian fundamentalists, other species of condemner, and the vulgar laws of infection. That the Gates must now be closed again leaves us with the onerous task of clean-up, and the trials of absorption... how to live with oneself, after 'sin'? How to become once more 'clean'? How to purge all the dirty Knowledge? This impossible task, too great even for our clever Doctors of Sex, is one of the neurotic convolutes that shall ever ensnarl our Syphilization.

The first Perversion is the pleasure of sex as diverted from the intent to procreate. Yet few deny that without this diversion life itself would be a squalid bore, no arts but the 'art' of raising the spawn, of eating and industry to support the spawn. To refuse this dull round is to become perverse. As one flowers in the singular – neurotic, psychotic, or triumphant – we create ourselves anew, and not in another's flesh but in our own. But the Pervert again has the horrific Responsibility to live up to the imperative that this new Freedom commands. He must not only create himself anew, but he must create himself Good. His mortal error – to fail to breed – must be translated into a metaphor for Redemption. Yet even in this self-redeeming strength we shall not know ourselves 'whole' – nor 'pure'. These absurd Ideals must be banished as inhuman torture-devices. The best one may achieve is the loss of the erosive self-hatred society would ever inflict upon We of Pervert cast. Self-judgement too shall be softened in the transformative process, and self-love reawakened.

The Mistress is often called upon not so much to inflict more cruelty – recall she is never First Destroyer, and only Archetypically Cruel – as to stand as a witness to Cruelty's continuing effects within the suffering slave. Often the afflicted-in-sex requires nothing more than to catch a glimmer of her Overcoming Wisdom. As Goddess she stands above the fray, observing with pity the nightmare clinches of the human intercourse. In the case of Peter #132, we cast our eye upon him and his virulent Mother.

From the Dungeon Records, Case of Peter #132: client of twelve years, age 44, pale and undernourished. Computer-genius, math honours in college. Has always lived with his mother and claims she has never allowed him to date. Mother has recently increased her demands upon Peter as she is ill with terminal cancer. Normally exceedingly mild-mannered and polite, sometimes when under the influence of alcohol will carry on in the corridors, screaming and vilifying us, creating a public disturbance. He always calls to apologise after one of these fits. He has not been banned because of his sincere repentances.

Peter is virtually livid with the deepest self-loathing. His masochism seems innate, his submissiveness at times eloquent. The psychological need is for verbal abuse: utter contempt, even expressions of hatred. The fetish is for dirt: the bottom of shoes and garbage pails, spittle, urine, dirty towels, used Kleenexes of any description. The physical masochism is relatively mild, he would be scratched or clawed or lightly trodden upon. In his drunken release he has shouted that we have not hurt him 'enough', this having a somewhat sarcastic ring to it.

July 1993: Peter called to cancel his session with Mistress Venuskat, saying his bank-machine card would not work. Venuskat insisted he still not fail to bring her headache medicine. He swore he had not dreamed of forgetting, had the pills and would be right over. When we opened the door, he stood before us in a hieratic pose of adoration, like some Egyptian statue: arms upraised, elbows together, hands in an attitude of prayer. Poised between his worshipful fingers was the bottle of Advil. He remained fixed so, with eyes tightly shut, as we plucked the pills from the altar, thanked him, and closed the door. Through the spy-hole we noted he retained his pose for some moments, before solemnly moving off.

September 1993: we are relieved to know his mother has finally died. Caught him waiting outside in the street for Mistress Ianna and asked how he was feeling. He stood up like a child at school and gave his report: only the most respectful and proper expressions of grief. His colour was better and he looked younger, already the 'tone' is improving without the mother's influence over him. He worships her mightily still but perhaps he will begin to make a motion towards having some relationship, however tragic the issue may be. His depressed air seemed feigned.

Terence Sellers

After his usual filthifying, shoe-laving, hideous gobbling, *et cetera*, he put forth to Mistress Ianna that it was now the time and place for him to undergo yet greater besmirchments. Or rather, "the greatest" – coprophagi. Of course she would not grant it – what he called 'the ultimate' – not only because few can 'produce' upon demand, but because the Mistress sensed he would not benefit from that further branding. She ended his session with a monologue on the ways and means of such feasts, assuring him he would have to 'earn the privilege' of such an intimate devourment. But we agreed that we will never grant it. With his mother gone, now there is a chance he might begin to shed some of the layers of his great self-loathing. Recommend possible infantilism session: regress him, find 'Mom', be Mom, try to root her out. Peter has always refused bondage, but it could have salutary effect: restrain his body and see if some aggression might be provoked, without the use of alcohol. Let him strain against the force of the woman's control. Would definitely help his tone which is already tending towards a more active mode. Maintain 'phone-contact, even if he does not come in for sessions.

Dear little Peter, let us stop then the infernal engines. First we shall mark off the delineations of your especial Evil, your criminal lust... Your body tells you what to do, does it not? It controls you, and you just follow... the Evil is therefore in your body! We Superiors – your Dominatrix, your Master – are here to control your body for you. We shall restrain it, make it quiet again. (But as we know your darkest secret, are we not ourselves imbued with this Evil you expel?) You cannot see how we do it, only that it is done. We effect our exorcism by a mere sleight-of-hand, as we all become actors, portray again your trauma at First Repression, and work to eject the psychic waste. The health of your body may follow – may not. Much depends on constitution, how degenerated you have become, how fixated and incapable of change, and the degree and firmness of your self-love.

Descend into our Paradise; Ascend in unbearable Knowing; go through with this Trial without too much lingering along the way over the fatal blooms.

the little history of walter #4: searching for an angel

My first encounter with domination was in the late 70s, on the second floor of an apartment building a few blocks north of the then-Barclay Hotel. A rather plain-looking, young brunette mistress with a bored expression told me to strip. After undressing, I was led to a vanity, where my face was made up and a wig added. I was then taken to the kitchenette near the front door. Ordering me to masturbate over the sink, the mistress whipped me with a belt sporadically. She then began taking calls, and while talking to prospective clients she would yell at me and they could hear the "crack" of the belt on my bare ass. It was an incredible turn-on. When I came, right in the sink, I was both embarrassed and exhilarated. But I never returned there.

Some years later, while visiting Manhattan, I discovered an establishment in the East 50's near Third Avenue. My first time, after undressing I told the mistress I wanted to wear panties and have her discover me lying on the bed masturbating. A few minutes later, she barged in, scolded me, and told me never again to touch myself without her permission. She then turned me into a sissy slave, upbraiding me constantly for wearing women's panties, pinching my nipples, and spanking my lingerie-clad bottom. We had quite a session. Another time, while I was on my knees before my mistress sitting on the side of the bed, a second mistress entered and sat down before me to discuss a matter with my mistress. She was very dominant and ordered me to worship her black stiletto heels while they talked. It made me unbelievably excited. It was years before I had the opportunity to experience the ultimate fantasy of serving

Terence Sellers

two mistresses for an entire session.

After moving to the metropolitan area to work in Manhattan, I began visiting dungeons. After several sessions at a rather unkempt place in the West 20's and a clean but uninspiring spot in the East teens, I found paradise on the eighth floor of a narrow building on 23rd Street just off Park Avenue South. Thus began an eight year odyssey that continues to this day. The main dungeon included a raised chair used as a throne, a large, black table with 4x4's at each corner and one horizontally centred above, all with strategically-placed I-hooks, a winch-driven suspension device, a rack, large mirrors, one table and chair and an adjoining bathroom. Across the hallway was the telephone room, beyond which was a much smaller and modestly equipped supplemental dungeon.

In an early session, my mistress turned out to be the proprietor, who then went by the name of Mistress Angel. A full-bodied, well-endowed redhead with striking blue eyes, Mistress Angel was and is stern and yet warm, and very exotic. I have served her one or more times each year, usually alone but occasionally in tandem with a second mistress. She now goes by the name Mistress Sterling to new slaves, but remains Mistress Angel to me, and presumably other long timers.

Early on, after several scheduling mishaps, I was given my own number and became Walter #4, so the phone attendant would know I was a dependable regular. After serving a number of mistresses for several years, I began seeing a beautiful slim blonde mistress named Sabrina regularly. She loved leather and discovered, as did I, my deep-seated leather fetish. From time to time, she would let me smell her leather outfits and never fail to remark on my many-faceted reactions. Just when she had admitted to a Size 4 and I had finally screwed up my courage to figure out a way to personally take her to buy a black leather outfit at the North Beach store at Madison and 66th Street, which she had said was her favourite spot, she left. As must happen in such professional circumstances, it was without explanation, but I felt a real void.

While I was trying to adjust to new, and very qualified, mistresses,

Angel introduced me to a newcomer, Marlene, and asked me if I would be willing to be her first client, promising to come back for the end of the session. It was an interesting and certainly worthwhile session, for how often does a slave have the opportunity to serve a brand new mistress, and in this case a well-trained and certainly enthusiastic one. Mistress Angel's appearance at the end made it an unforgettable experience, especially when she smothered me for the first time! I have probably served Mistress Marlene at least a dozen times since, and she has proven to display all the potential that Mistress Angel saw in her from the beginning.

Several years ago, the dungeon was moved to West 20th Street, which was less than totally satisfactory, so a subsequent move was arranged to 43rd Street near 8th Avenue, and an upcoming move is likely in 1995. As is almost universally true, however, it is the human quality, not location, that makes the difference, and Mistress Angel has established a standard that will continue to attract persons such as me wherever she and her very able and professional associates decide to reside. Total trust is a rare commodity in this crazy world in which we live. For those of us who, for reasons often difficult to truly comprehend, need to give ourselves completely in submission to a mistress we respect, Mistress Angel represents the best that there is and can be. I look forward to continue serving her and those she carefully selects in the years to come.

In the service of Mistress Angel,
Walter #4

PART THREE

"LAST LECTURES": OUR POOR PROGNOSIS

the pervert vs. the neurotic vs. the straight

I realized early on in my vocation as a Dominatrix how universally I was despised, and for two reasons: not only was I socially aligned with the prostitute, but I had assumed the Superior mode. My Work being illegitimized by the law and by psychiatry, I faced pariahdom, as well as the difficulties inherent in the Work. Even those who worshipped me within the ritual psychodrama could hold me in a certain horror as a type of "bad woman". Yet I had the gall to go on believing I was a truly Superior person, and would not submit to the 'straight' idea that perversity was a thing to be 'cured', and its expression avoided at all costs. Under these influences it is no wonder I was at times beset by fear, vague panic at the thought of some hideous retribution on its way against me. I understood that certain of my 'friends' awaited with certainty just this bad end. But as in time passing I prospered and strengthened myself in my convictions, I am able to enjoy their rancour... though the bad days do come and I am tormented by a paranoid 'certainty' that the forces inherent in the dark influence I wield and evoke will eventually drive me mad.

But with the exaltations of power shall I not suffer too its persecutions? To overcome all obstacles – to consider one's degraded status in the world a mere error of current morality to be vindicated by posterity – to provide consoling Knowledge to my fellow pariah – and in the integrity of answering only to one's interior law and reason shall one at last realize happy desire, as it evolves from within as both attainable and Ideal – we shall at last live bravely, and thus *freely*.

This is of course the formula for psychosis – *that moral law is not for such as I.* Should I fall silent, and fail to articulate this darkness for you, then you may become wary of me. But, until then, you may read me.

To have a normal sex-life is an ideal enough for the average straight person. Let them attain to this convention with all their souls. Let them be reconciled to what would be for us a compromised existence. (Indeed they never fail to assert that compromise is a sign of 'maturity'!) My own brief foray into the precincts of a 'normal' relationship assured me forever of its incompatibility with my Imperial Being.

Straight women we pervert women find profoundly dull and even annoying. They may briefly evince some curiosity of our Knowledge of the underside of 'respectability'. Yet as they edge closer to us, too close, will come the reaction – of course they will despise us. That men may become beasts and indeed *often prefer their bestiality to anything angelic* is an insufferable vision to these clean wives of husbands; that violent, disgusting, insane things might arouse men *more* than a wife's hallowed body is too awful a reality for them to long countenance. Unable to bear this black shadow of sex they wrench their eyes away, kill their curiosity, renew their restraints upon all men and any 'experimentation', and fling the 'filth' back upon *those women.* Should their man dare to engage in that horror, he will be flung in the trash with the vile Demonesses. Rather than live as lonely rejects, many men will thus lie. Straight women, in refusing to accept the male sexuality in its entirety without condemnation, forbid Love to Perversity and sanction the pariah class of pervert women. But our continuing existence affirms the imperfection of their straight Ideal.

Let us examine more closely our terms, *straight, pervert* and *neurotic* in this context. To be *straight* is to conform in entirety to the convention of the Ideal Normal. Its requirements are that one be adamantly heterosexual, preferably married, procreative, monogamous, and engaging with one's partner-for-life in standard penile intromission *ad vaginam.* All variations upon this formula will be considered abnormal: either *perverted,* or, as per the *neurotic* mentality, sick.

The *pervert* has the courage of his convicted desire. He does not ponder with any deep concern the societal onus upon him, more preoccupied with the *how to* than the *why* of his nature. He fully appreciates its mechanisms; that its *why* may never be answered does not impede him from every attempt to know his pleasure. He understands that *the Will to the Why achieves a loss in pleasure*, and fails to pursue this neurotic mode. He seeks always the consent of his love-object (if it be human), restrains himself until his desire can be safely expressed, and avoids any situation where he might be branded a criminal. Or, he may *not* restrain himself. It may be that after the sexuality has been thwarted too often, even maimed by violent disapproval, the thrill of criminality may be all that is left to it. In the service of our strange pleasures, still we must not invent a new morality, not mistake freedom with that old crime: *I allow myself to do whatever I want.* If we cannot devise ingenious formulae to aid in our realization of desire, if that grey and marginal room within the larger society cannot be found, we must remain mere fantasists, and not cultivate a slyness nor a brutality towards the achievement of that pleasure.

The pervert might often be called sick – *but he never passes this destructive judgement upon himself.* The *neurotic*, on the other hand, is nothing *but* sick. The unusual desires he harbours in his body and mind he might consider as a cancer of the soul. Or perhaps it is an alien entity, taken up residence inside him. Or maybe he is the victim of some unremembered abuse, forced on him in childhood. An evil spell was no doubt muttered over his crib as a baby – exorcism is in order, to 'eradicate' vile desire. There is every excuse made to explain why he is the poor slave of all these deleterious influences ever working upon him. It is anything but something he himself is responsible for – no, he is not in control, *not* in control of his body.

        "How can I consider the hideous responsibility!" we hear him shriek, "that I may never know orgasm but under the heel of a snickering bitch? That pleasure for me is only in the spray of a pissing butch-Master? That only when beaten to within an inch of my life does that life have any meaning?"

He breaks down weeping, "No, it cannot be! I must be normal, somewhere inside, somewhere inside of me is that innocent person again, who doesn't need this vileness!"

Thereupon the neurotic dances attendance upon the definitions psychiatry has made for him. The psychoanalyst, acting upon the mind of the patient, may alter it for the worse. We Superior ones view any attempt to change the mind of another as a highly suspect enterprise. The neurotic adorns himself with the complex labels of sickness and acquires their exotic vocabulary. Perhaps he suffers from *dissociative disorder*, a species of neurosis whereby the bodily state is a vague arena open to interpretation... or his personality may be discovered to be *schizoid*, unplanted in reality, prone to cracking, double-takes and *multiple personality*. This last is a convenient trash-bin to throw the horrifying perversities into, "I didn't do it, that evil 'Jason' did!"

Or perhaps he may be in the chronic stage of an *obsessive-compulsive neurosis*, wherein this form of sexuality has become rigidly instituted to the exclusion of all others. Most likely he partakes of *psychopathy*, for only someone with a defective conscience could have evolved to behave in such inhuman fashion... or it may be a simple *absence of neural effect*, whereby one is physically numb to certain good ideas of normal life due to the failure of the brain chemicals to exude at the proper time, causing neurons to fire at inappropriate moments. All this terminology points to the state of *incipient insanity*, and may be considered as conducive of insanity in the thinking being.

The failure of imagination that compels the neurotic to submit to such control is quite 'normal' in our modern age. (All such language is steadfastly avoided by the Superior except as a mode of irony.) This vocabulary describes states as observed from the outside, as observations from the sufferer must be diseased. This practice of paying no mind to the words of 'madmen' is a pertinently modern disease.

The terminology used by psychiatry to describe the paraphiliac are very powerful in their assigned function of devising a control over another person. Mistress Angel favours the rather more blunt, evocative instruments of early psychiatry for use in certain verbal-abuse scenarios. For example, the term 'morally insane' has always been one of her special favourites.

The proper use of epithets, the creation of a sexualized language, will *cathartically* humiliate the sufferer, define his pleasurable insanity, and create a comfort zone of moral grey – where he is not, however, *protected*, but where he is punished; and as he is being reviled for his 'crime', the very 'crime' itself is allowed sexual expiation. His repentance gives him total *jouissance*...

With self-knowledge may come an ironic detachment and in time a loss of fear. Controls are confounded if one has some idea of the private meaning of such inner states. No control may dictate terminology; the description of the inner state is taken up by the individual. The actions pertaining thereunto will receive no judgement from outside themselves, except from those whom he regards as his equals, that is, at a similar degree of advancement. Aghast, the psychiatrist throws up his hands – here we have before us a true pervert – an incurable! Yes, we are the incurables, among those who have discovered your control is a sort of confidence game.

Those in the psychiatric profession may, and will function as incorrect sadists. They have too much influence over certain ultra-influenceables. Neurotics historically have little recourse against psychic invasion. What torture could be more precise: "Your art is but a symptom... a stylistic aberration upon a deep sickness..." (Some critics have agreed.)

Those Incorrect Ones will always be pleased that their neurotic is such a desperate creature. That this sufferer hates himself when he feels pleasure is considered a *healthy* sign. Because his pleasure is *sick*, you see. His self-rejection is a sign of healing. What utter perversity!

Yet the worst of sadists or psychiatrists could not invent more complex tortures than those the neurotic sadomasochist imposes upon himself. In him, both sadism and masochism have become an active, wholly internalized force: the masochist grovels before the sadist, begging to be allowed to experience his only pleasure. The sadist within says, "No." Then, the masochist disobeys, breaks out in rebellion, and indulges full frenzy. After this, the sadist is there (they never go away) attacking the masochist as sick – filthy – disgusting. All these judgments are fully, humbly accepted; but they serve not to change the behaviour, but to make the next submission all the more piquant. This violent oscillation between self-indulgence and self-punishment usually occurs within the four walls of a solitary bedroom.

Thus too the neurotic kneels before the critical world, begging for forgiveness, unable to ever achieve its approval as long as he remains as sick as he is. The pervert however stands as the sadist to the world, full of pride in his terrible 'madness', satanic in his arrogant *I Want and I Will*. The best continually transform and translate themselves, unable in the end to be placed in any category. Self-knowledge is their crown and their achievement. 'Should' is not a word that the Superior one allows within their precincts. The neurotic is a pre-eminent 'Christian', forever sinful and forever repentant. He is appalled to be discovered in his crime, and grovels before *I Should Not I Cannot*. The neurotic is assured of the pity, and mild disgust, of the straights; but both are terrorized by the pervert, whose appetite is only whetted by a persecution.

Psychoanalysis can reveal to the neurotic the delicate machinery of his desires. This knowledge may then either inspire more fear in him against their realization, or it may awaken him to the relief of self-acceptance. Most analysts insist upon the need for sublimation in some form, towards the highest control of desire. Why this foolish warning against any expression of certain desires? Because they have 'determined' that such expressions result in a degeneration of the faculties? As though the faculties are not subject to degeneration in time? We might save ourselves for God, yet go to seed and wither in any event.

At this point in your analysis, foolish neurotic, it is essential that you recover some pride. Attempt some safe means of expression – invent! Repression is not your solution. Such a means might be found in the realm of the professional Doctors of Sex. We provide a padded zone between repression and criminal outburst. There may your arcane passions be brought to at least some grey light, to confront the matter and drain it of potentially explosive force. In that, we provide an inestimable, if secret, service to society, and are thus, to that end, really straighter than straight.

the rank odour of the pure

"What does it mean when a philosopher pays homage to the ascetic ideal? He seeks to gain release from a torture."[1]

To gain release from the torture of sex... of being always desirous, of needing others who are not there... of waiting for some god to save us. In the long hard silence of our hunger, through the orderly minutes of pain, might we yet pass through perpetuities of joy?

Let us make a study of how to deny ourselves that 'greatest' of all pleasures... as we once goaded ourselves on to highest indulgence. Let us assure ourselves that we might be very good – as we had been so evil. For we debauchees are possessed too of our own religious vocation. We too revolve about that moral nut, that suffering might be good – and pleasure evil. In these revolutions do we find some detachment. To refine ourselves 'celibately resolved' is our religious art. Neither sated, nor frustrated, and somewhat hermaphroditic we have accepted with equanimity every confessed fantasy. Like a priest – yet we know more than priests, and thus are more suited to receiving confessions than those dank hypocrites in their unrevealing attire.

We may consider celibacy in two aspects: the first being that fabled pure and self-contained state; the second as a form of *libertinage.*

Oddly, the fragile, over-cerebral, pasty sort of being, one barely able to survive the ordeal of erection, is not most worthily suited to

---

[1] Friedrich Nietzsche.

Terence Sellers

attain to our ideal of flawless celibacy. (Such as these *benefit* from a frequent infusion of energy from without.) It is the sanguine temper, vigorous and abundantly sensuous, which easily adapts to the celibate state. Their forcible, robust energy guarantees it to be always vitally at hand for usage. They may take hold of this thriving and plant it vitally elsewhere, where they wish. Their sublimations are always passionate, they have a talent for self-control. *What does it mean to pay homage to the ascetic ideal?* To find another type of pleasure exactly as satisfying as the physical.

It may surprise some to know that an advanced de Sadean sensualist would embrace celibacy as an exaltation upon sexuality. We have placed it in the service of our greatest pleasure, of course: sadomasochistic oscillation – as slight starvation does add *piquancy* to a feast at hand. But more than this mere temporary effect, celibacy is an imperative to the rigours of hygiene – psychic as well as the physical. Too often we are drained and exhausted by the weaker beings who vampirically crave after us. To be, as it were, a sexual dynamo, capable of recharging partners in multitudes... we are as a vital source for others, and are constantly pursued. It is so delightful to partake of us. Too, to refrain from a conjugal sex may afford one much relief and strength again, as constant supplication, usage, love, attacks, *et cetera*, all in the final analysis render up little happy issue. The sublimated Will, however, may engender pleasure upon pleasure without enervation.

We libertines from time to time do nostalgically require the imposition of celibate discipline. We like to remember what it was like to really want – to be hungry. We are capable of a self-control others are not. Under control that is wise all may enjoy a serene self-sufficiency, but being of a lively, naturally regenerative physicality, we are well familiar with that stalwart force of sex, and can draw in our peculiarly conscious way upon Ourselves for what We Will: if We Will, and when We Will – or not.

This is our celibacy as a 'pure and self-contained state' – We do not seek to shut down, close off, or seal up the organs of generation. The techniques of sublimation are not for all, are a matter of esoteric study. Tantric yoga may hold some keys, but experimentation is essential. Those who pursue this course may have the highest of goals, creative aims. As we commence a work that requires sustained intellectual capacity, the banal outlet of sexual intercourse will waste the instrument. We too understand that certain acute indulgences, certain debilitating emotional exercises may sometimes not be recovered from. Indeed it is so: you may 'never love again!' Thus to observe an economy assures the Operator some power reserve for the years to come.

A common abuse of celibacy in its aspects of libertinage we find manifest in the Roman Catholic priesthood. These are men 'perfectly pure' – a title even we of strictest libertine denial do not try to assume. We may ask how a young, possibly virginal priest may honestly pontificate on the evils of untrammelled sex? How does he know that could be so?

"Lust, daughter of opulence and superiority, cannot be treated except by people of a certain stamp... except by individuals, who blessed by nature to begin with, are also sufficiently blessed in fortune to have tried themselves what they trace for us..."[1]

Excess of ignorant self-restraint, in the service of sex-hatred, dams up and perverts the natural energies from their appointed course. That priests might be the most unnatural of men should therefore not surprise anyone. We have certainly discovered that their holy retreats are the seed-beds of some very secret loves. Every hunger will have its day, and upon the young and unwilling (and so desirable) they fall, without asking permission. Seduction and secretion are the two bywords of these falsely holy ones. In truth the mask of the celibate is a perfect hiding place for the lusting pederast. That other varieties of perversion may flourish in convents and seminaries we of course have no objection to, only that improperly stoppered sexuality may explode its vessel, scattering a filthy shrapnel. Children in the care of priests have been coerced and forcibly contained for sexual service. In one worst case, a group of priests systematically corrupted every boy in their care. Nightly one was chosen for the priests' satanic revels. Then the boys were

---

[1] The Marquis de Sade, *Letters*.

---

terrorized by tales of the punishments due them from God, for being the inspirers of the sexual thoughts. Which to be sure is the truth. Still, the good priests told their boys they had known the desire to rape them as *forced* upon them – by the rampant lustiness of 'bad boys'!

Holy resolve may at best succeed in rendering up for our disgusted delectation the priest and nun as automaton. Sexless, inhuman functionaries of a Church too long prospering under an imposed and specious guilt. Alas for the punishments guaranteed we sinners, we poor weak debauchees! *Those who suffer become cruel* [1]. The rank odour of these 'pure ones' is the secret of the whited sepulchre – why need we smell of the festering lust of their frustrated souls? We know the sight of a naked body 'enrages' them – a peculiar reaction – quite unnatural. And it is a fault in we naked ones if we cringe and cover up before their putrid scorn, if we do not meet their spittle with a laugh and flaunt the happy excess of refusing for all time their long affliction of shame.

---

[1] Wilhelm Stekel.

---

bloodshed, one of the pastimes of humanity: angel vs. satan

But how can the sadistic instinct, whose aim it is to injure the object, be derived from Eros, the preserver of life?[1]

There is a known excitement upon the flow of blood: that red colour (oh lovely red), the terror in it, *of the mysterious interior revealed.* We *ought not* to be so thrilled, *ought not* to admit we so love the flow. Even We, for whom 'ought' and 'should' are not words, even We agree that to read and watch and savour the trickling away of the thick and precious essence, should not be too much indulged. We *ought* always to say we are appalled... and yet the thrill is there and will *always* be there.

(O readers of the future, can you conceive of these times, where we might haggle the issues of preferring, or not, to have a conscience? Where we interpret how delightful – or not – a particular form of mayhem might be?)

It does not matter if we have not actually caused a physical death – though we all have, squashing bugs – for in serving as an audience to mayhem in books and films *we have purposed Death.* As with the chicken-killing dog, *there has now been developed a taste for blood...* as again that animal pleasure we crave, to see and know blood again. Is it any longer in our power to repress it? To well-control 'the dog'? Like the dog, ought we be taken out and

---

[1] Freud, *Beyond The Pleasure Principle.*

Terence Sellers

shot, lest we 'kill' – and kill again?

(We are now a nation, a very *world of murderers*. We sanction an eternal flow of blood. Because Death feels *too delightful*.) There is more pleasure in thinking upon Death than 'ought to be' humanly possible!

We repeat: one ought always to be appalled – because to admit, or even imply that one might feel otherwise – that one *applauds* the flow – is to present a face that is only detestable. (As is most of humanity – author not excluded.)

Your popular imagination fastens upon the extremities of sadistic joy: homicide, infanticide, and kidnapping; tortures prolonged for days, videotaped for later delectation; all the varied torments of sex-slavery to the sexually repellent, *et cetera* (yes, my readers, there is an infinity of death; ever inventive are the insane). All these perpetrations of non-consensual *submission* may be gazed upon in newspapers, books, in film, and effectively loathed. Staring and loathing... loathing and staring. So is the loathing a kind of lie, that we must lie?... for we cannot admit we love... there seems a very wide, greyly flickering, strangely depthless area where we, as audience, might linger... in a place impalpable to some of the senses... these are the approaches to Death, wherein we are attended by the larvae of torment.

(And why *should* blood be allowed to course *only* selfishly inside the body? Why not that lovely flow upon our hands, into the ground? When properly spilt, is blood even wasted? We desire that deeper bonding with the earth, to die and sink into Her. Secretly we want to be pressed: one's life for the sake of another's – or, another one's life, given up to one's own. That honoured atavism – sacrifice – uses human blood towards its highest communions.)

Some few may understand what erotic violence is... a pleasure the Master-Mistress delights to inflict... and how, when we fall, we do fall upon *the willing victim*. This is the mystery, the infernal paradox of sadomasochism – that there are those who desire, nay even *design* their cross and their delight. But how can even We of the

Theatrical Dungeon fully comprehend – and, over time, stomach –
the thrill of that mystic approach unto Death?

Enter the Theatrical Dungeon: here your violence is translated into
a 'psychodrama'. This is achieved by means of a rather outmoded
form of therapy that had its moment in the 1960's – 'implosion
therapy'. Your worst fears – the most humiliating desire – the most
dire thoughts – are evoked and made flesh. The Master-Mistress is
all-powerful, a daemonic, enlivening force. Confess! The Mistress-
Master directs the playlet; the enslaved groans upon the boards.
Both undergo – through dramatic play – the tragi-comedy of their
psycho-sexual traumata. Both enscript the scene; the Mistress-Master
edits with the cruel nicety of the Director. The grand dénouement
is the orgasm of the patient.

(We can imagine the problem a conventional therapist might have
with such a therapy... we too founder upon the *insatiability* of the
masochist for certain nightmares – their love for things disgusting
often seems bottomless – are we alleviating or merely indulging? –
it often seems the desires become more pronounced, more 'insane',
worse – how could the doctors risk their insurance policies? We who
are not bowed down by this unneedful responsibility are there,
however, to see the pleasure through – as long as the self-
knowledge may take – a lifetime perhaps. And we are, as well,
permitted to enjoy the erotic spectacle.)

Part of the 'mystique' of the sadomasochistic engagement is that the
desire to be Other than what one is – to be one's Opposite – to be
as if Dead – these approaches to Deadly sex through erotic pain are
'cleaned up' – made relatively rational – made *artful* – made into
theatre in our 'Dungeon'. The artistry of professionally inflicted
violence has evolved, over a few decades, into a true refinement
upon human violence. We Practitioners comprehend that violence
may be *etherealized out* of the grosser physical inflictions/afflictions
into a *purely psychic effect*. This is achieved through a relatively
rational psychodramatic *action*, whose purpose is a freeing one, and
effectively leads to cathartic orgasm. *This is our Divine Control over
the infernal blundering instinct-to-Death.*

(But to become the owner of another human being is a pleasure incontrovertible. This is the essence of the sadistic pleasure. For we Sadic professionals it is most often a fantasy – and approach – and thus not the full crime. The soul of the pure crime Sadism is total possession – which only true bloodshed can satisfy. By his gratifications, the killer gains again and 'again' (and he *is* regressed) – a most primeval power – knows that peculiar and innate strength of the greatest animal that is: a human. An 'uncivilised', seemingly 'pure' vitality throbs in our veins – as the scent hits us. Not even the flow of semen compares with the rich pulsing blood flowing across our hands, into the ground, an admittedly brief ownership. So might we stand imperially apart from the decadent, weakling modern as we feel his body dying beneath ours in ecstatic embrace.)

<u>Monologue: To The Murderer's Beloved</u>

> I love you – I want you – I want to control you.
> Now I own you – I own your life.
> You are no longer just you – you are part of me.
> I make you into myself.
> You are my life – you own my life – you control me.
> I own your life – I control your life –
> *Don't try to get away!*
> You won't submit – you don't love me –
> *Now I have to kill you.*
> When I kill you, you will be mine forever.
> No chance then of ever escaping ME.
> I love you therefore
> you must die.

(But nothing you can do can stop the blood from flowing. The blood that is spilled and pouring out even as we speak – permeates the air and has reached our nostrils. This scent produces excitement... a kind of ecstatic trance. In especial temperaments we might remark *a happy phrenzy*. We have seen its free coursing, sunk with it into a suspension in time, where life began its departure... we watch... we watch...)

The homicidal sadist requires no intellectual concurrence with his victim, nor any conscious emotional attachment. They need only the body of any victim now, to grip the flesh of the hated one, thrill to see their helplessness. The stream of happy desire may now rush towards its vile, unnecessary end.

(We who have learned to savour the erotic flow will not have Our lust restrained! No legislation or electric chair will ever deny to Some their exaltation. One might conquer another... pleasure is Death is all too possible... yes and semen *has* been found floating in a puddle of victim's blood.)

Why are those who kill professionally both greatly honoured, and abhorred? (Soldiers and hit men are *needed.* They act to confirm the power of the government – or a *capo di tutti capi* – who dare to order bloodshed in their name.) Why are the means of Death subject to so much research and refinement? (The military-industrial complex churns on, oblivious to all threats of peace. Arcane devices are sold expensively in sex-shops, created to inflict one specific, exquisite, exciting pain.) Why *can* torture and the refinements of Death become the subject of a morally neutral research? (Because, on the deepest level, *murder is a normal human activity.*) Why are war-zones now called 'theatres'? (To increase that sense of pleasurable detachment necessary to feel one is in total control.) Why can the average serial killer appear normal to his neighbours, laugh, eat well and heartily after a kill? And what if the entire human race was to be cut away from the face of the earth by a few starkly clear-eyed killers? And why is it that this would not matter?

(The more wildly, cruelly, satanically we indulge ourselves, without that annoying consideration for some weakling's shivering feelings, so much the more might we devour and exploit thereby, towards the end of our deserved grandeur. Humanistic theory to the contrary – that we might only live *happily* when good and kind and gently civilised – we have thrust aside all fear, and in the wake of new and rampant prosperance, achieve *domination* over the bits of quailing humanity we might have left alive... until the day, of course, when we are hunted down like mad dogs and shot.)

Terence Sellers

a profound disgust for things human

For the one who has been hidden; for the one who will reveal – We must apply the cruel consolation of Our Discipline. We suffer, but do not die in the dredging up of horrors from their bed of pain. Suffer We *all* – but never senselessly.

For We have a Reason for the pain!

As We continue to page over the vast extent of human suffering, we are convinced of one thing – and that is pain's constancy. As vast an indifference to it abides in most persons: the safe and normal ones. But no-one is safe from the Maw. Even those who meet and greet it daily get the fear: that there might be no Reason, might be no Order, that even karma's Maya, no such thing as fateful deserving. Such as We assuredly dread, *vertige vers la Nausée vielle*, grip a swayback seat at the cosmic vomitorium.

A profound disgust for all torments inflicted, and suffered, in the name of Love. Wives against husbands, brother over sister, children athwart their weeping parents, all mesh and meld and conglomerate flesh, inspiring in the best of sensibilities deep aversion to humanity. But what better way, to be forever remembered, than to inflict Trauma? Is there even such a thing, if there are no longer any Ideals of human love, no reason for the procreative imperative... no hope for a regeneration of a true morality? To be, needs must submit – *We?* Is not our violence – merely hygiene?

What better way to be remembered than to impress Trauma? The criminal designs that this should be so. *So you think you can ignore me, do you? If you pretend I don't exist, I will just disappear – right? You have this contempt – very well I shall leave my MARK upon you, never to be. erased. You will be mine, you will be a part of what you loathe, yes as you share my pain, fool, and never, never forget.*

I have developed over the years the most intense interest in the works and workings of the seriously deranged. I admit I have enjoyed pathology wherever I found it. Yet I came too to the end of a certain blithe toleration, when I acquired a book of photographs for use in the training of the forensic pathologist: one who makes a study into the meaning of wounds.

Not one of the pictured mutilations had been caused by the act of a green lizard-monster, alien from space, or hell-bound demon. Each gash and tear, every bruise and mark was made by the hand of a human being – acting upon the flesh of sister and brother fellow-man.

Was this the most serious horror of it? Or was it the cool, scientific boredom of tone, as it passed alongside the *tableaux mourants?* Was it that assumed familiarity with nightmarish torment – an eye almost colder than the eye that victimized? Alterations may come to pass within one who studies such subjects. What might be the design of one who would be expert in the handiwork of the violent?

I admit I gorged myself upon the colour photographs, growing sicker at each passing page, unable to believe how long the book had become... Yet I could not stop looking, I wanted to see it all, I wanted to be able to take it.

a cluster of bruises and scratches, arranged in crescentic manner, on the left arm of a woman who was murdered. They may have been produced by the fingers and nails of the assailant, as he gripped her from behind.

the partially cleaned bones of the body of an old man who disappeared from a mental hospital. He was a known depressive who had vanished into the woods, never to be seen alive again. When the vegetation had withered in the Winter, these remains were revealed. Note that the blade of the scapula has been eaten away by rats; the curved rat-bites can just be discerned.

the chest of a man stabbed twice with a butcher knife. There has been some dissection of the tissues of the chest wall around the site of wounding. Dissection of the rib cage on one side shows the various structures through which the knife passed. It is useful to dissect the body with the weapon in position, if the track of the wound is to be clearly ascertained.

She who pulls the weapon from the wound knows more of Death than she who used one.

It is always worth remembering that most murders have a sexual content of one sort or another and to keep a careful watch for anything that might be unusual. Detergents have been poured in victim's mouths, objects of various sort inserted and subsequently removed from vagina and rectum. Seminal and blood stains may be found in unexpected places, and so on.

She who pulls the knife from its wound-bed can never be the one who fixed it there.

I read the book through, gazing with avidity upon the grisly human remains. Quite happy to see that the body will one day, yes, be over! Quite satisfied that I could stomach through this truest show of sadism.

Hypothermia fatality – this not infrequently happens in cold bedrooms when the infant is inadequately clothed and the bedding insufficient to keep it warm. The purple marks are due to sludging of the blood in the vessels.

But twenty-four hours later, not having slept, I was still crouched upon the toilet, retching. Anything I ate for the next three days came up, unable to evade a phantom scent in my sinuses, rot, unable to remove the sight of a child's eviscerated ass, used beyond belief... or the remnants of vicious sex, vaginal squalor, unspeakable depth of the cavities – every type of food an insect could want.

Why flinch to see what is underneath – sinew and fat, coil of intestine, what lives and moves and gives us being? Why loathe the sight of the exposed human heart, still beating? Our interiors were once forbidden knowledge, for centuries a taboo laid upon surgeons which made them criminal in their design to dissect, open up the corpse. (Perhaps one day we who delve into our sex will be granted absolution, no longer condemned as psychotic immoralists.)

A specialized faculty of mind has predisposed me to such investigations: no real horror of the details of decay (initiated fully in the vomitorium); desire to attain to that scientific callous and clarity; fascination with the abnormal; intolerance of the ideals of human love and generation (for all ties may be severed, nothing is sacred).

I myself do not so much shrink from love as am I perpetually bored by it. This is a pain I have felt so often it no longer holds any novelty. When things go particularly roughly, I go out of town, lock myself in the remote location, and die a little, into clean solitude.

Thus I take my part in punishment.

a deep incised wound on the neck produced suicidally using a cut-throat razor. The larynx has been incised but does not extend sufficiently posteriorly to divide the carotid arteries or jugular veins. Death in this case was due to multiple haemorrhages and from inhalation of blood into the damaged larynx. There are no tentative incisions here.[1]

---

[1] All quotes from A *Colour Atlas Of Forensic Pathology*, by G. Austin Gresham (Wolfe, 1975).

Terence Sellers

If only women would stop being the hopeless, hapless victims of history and took charge of it like Messalina of Rome, Theodora of Byzantium, Mrs. Marcos of the Philippines, Madame Nhu of Viet-Nam and Empress Farah of Iran (before the latter two fell from power because their husbands were stupid fools), then men would be happier so they could stop pretending to be the hunters and the macho characters of history, accept the gelded role and perform tasks necessary to make the women pleased, happy, content and comfortable. Only through pain can man achieve peace, glory and fulfilment. You – Goddess – understand that!

Messalina used to masturbate men to death and then in the final act when they were totally spent from nine or ten ejaculations, she gleaned a Sharp-Hot-Jagged Knife from one of her assistants and one can hear the screams today in Rome if one listens attentively.

Masturbate a man once and he will thank you and feel pleasure; never let up on your grip, pump away and he will in time feel no pleasure... ONLY PAIN. Messalina, the wife of Claudius, understood this and what a beauty she was... the perfect woman of the Gods!

Theodora of Byzantium roasted men alive in empty cow's skins over a roaring fire and enjoyed the festivity of screams with her girl friends and any servant who failed perfection today became tomorrow's entertainment.

In Medieval England, the young daughter of a Noble invented the Iron Maiden, a coffin-like device filled with nails, needles and pins and into it a man went for an afternoon's entertainment... I am sure many an orgasm was delightfully engaged in thanks to that imaginative waif of a girl who made sponges out of men.

In our own day, Mrs. Marcos, Madame Nhu and Empress Farah HELPED CREATE THE AURA OF TERROR IN THEIR COUNTRIES FOR THEY HAD TORTURE CHAMBERS WHERE THEY TOOK ENEMIES OF THE STATE WHO FOLLOWING DAYS OF SCREAMING, CREAMING AND SHRIEKING DISAPPEARED FOREVER.

In Nazi Germany, Ilsa, She Wolf of the infamous SS made

love to men but if the man ejaculated before Ilsa's orgasm, WOE unto him and he would not leave her chambers with all the anatomical parts he came in with; Irma Greese, whom the British hanged at Belsen Camp in 1944, took castrating men to the state of the art... so painfully long she made the men endure it. She also tortured women with large breasts while she foamed at the mouth, squeezed her thighs together and moaned exotically. She also devised the method of tying a woman's legs together at childbirth, thus killing the child and the mother in a most painful fashion.

Ilsa Koch skinned men's testicles while they were awake and made lamp shades with them... naturally, I am not advocating such a scenario but perhaps I have kindled a spirit in you to make such tortures (whenever possible) POSSIBLE!

I have always been fascinated by women who love to torture men... what motivates them, when did their desires start, what limits, if any, do they impose upon themselves or are there no limits, how do you know when you are going beyond a man's limits and endurance or do you ignore such feelings and strike them from your mind as you torture a man endlessly? I suppose in the long run, once he is naked, bound, racked, spread-eagled, vulnerable and exposed, it is his problem, not your's. What a sensual-erotic, sexual thought... a booted torturess leaning down over a racked, spread-eagled, arched-backed, sweating, screaming, shrieking, moaning, pleading, crying man, with a table next to him filled with the implements of pain and the woman having total control of his destiny, his pain and the future of his human parts. I am ready to go into my chamber of pain and suffer for you NOW!

You are certainly a beautiful woman, one worthy of a man's worship, adoration, lone and honour and I can imagine how heavenly it must be to spend hours naked before you, kissing, adoring, worshipping, and honouring your precious feet, your magnificent calves, your inviting thighs although the 'holy of holies' should always be covered as no slave is worthy to look upon such pleasure without first suffering hell for that honour. The man is the inferior being and should not be allowed relief unless the tortures bring them on or unless the mistress, in a truly erotic-sensual-magnanimous act of charity, decided to help bring the man to ejaculation but not before hours of teasing, tickling and near 'misses'. A few mistresses recently were involved in Prostitution... Never should a woman descend to that depth!

I am going into my chamber of pain soon, will spread my legs wide along the walls until they touch the floor which in time becomes very painful and then I will torture myself in your honour with pins, needles, hot items, in the and on the scrotal sac, whip the penis and place my cock ring with sharp points on: I will use heavy rubber bands with which to whack... the genitals; beat my penis and testicles (never to be referred to as cock and balls... too low class) with a heavy wet ruler; apply the hot lighter to various parts including the pubic hair which I also pluck out one by one (how sensuously painful and mind boggling) and will also place alligator clips on the tits and pull off. In front of me throughout these tortures is your photo and you are smiling down at me in an approving way although I realize it would be far more painful if you were performing the acts of pain. I scream your name and shriek for your orgiastic pleasure and hope the neighbours are watching 'DALLAS' and hear not a peep.

I hope you do not think me a pervert or nearing insanity... just curious as to the relationship between the torturess and the tortured. What binds them together, what do they feel as kindred spirits, what pleasures can they share together and how far will a man go to honour, worship, adore and suffer for a beautifully legged, full breasted, imaginative redhead-fiery... brunette... sultry... blonde... cool, aloof... mistress of pain and pleasure?

My favourite dream is the one where a man or men are on one side of a wall their penises and testicles protruding through openings in the wall into a hallway where Nazi and other torturesses patrol jabbing at the genitals with long sharp staves and of course relishing in hearing the reaction on the other side of the wall.

Sometimes these transmitters of pain sneak up on the man so the surprise is deafening with his screams for some men begin to cry and shriek just hearing the clicking of the boots and high heels on the hallway floor. A smashing scenario!

Another classic centres on the Victorian house (what else?) where the basement has been made into various torture chambers depending on what is to be done to the man and a conveyor device shuttles the men – naked and spread-eagled – from one chamber to the other until he is put on to a siding, helped onto the torture rack and it becomes his turn to bounce his body on the rack and his screams off the dungeon walls. He travels through each chamber before being chosen thus seeing what is going on in each room and some are on different levels so he gets the sensation of going downward and upward and in time it all becomes a swirl and he loses all sense of time, space and occurrence. The women are dressed in various coloured outfits... blue is novice and for beginners learning the trade... green is for achievers of the first step by passing a written exam on the pain points and parts of the male anatomy .. red is for passing the first physical torture application examination and black is conferred only after hours, weeks, and months if not years of learning and the passing of strenuous and vigorous examinations... both written and applied. Usually, the young women in blue are teenagers learning the craft of the mistresses and to the removing of the men from the various torture devices, arranging the implements and recording the goings-on. With determination, drive, imagination, verve, aggressiveness and hard work, in time they will achieve the highest goal... Mistress 1st rating which only one woman can achieve at one time... her word is law, her desires are immediately carried out... her tortures of the male so awe inspiring and all bow before her will. She wears the GOLD. So if ever a male sees a GOLD GODDESS coming at him, he is in for the hassle of his life... what is left of it. All the women, except those in blue, carry a whip on a hook on the right side of their outfit and a castration knife on the left side .. they are ready and willing to use these implements, no questions asked, no hesitations, no argument. When I dream these dreams, I usually awaken following an immense and intense ejaculation for the dream ends with a GOLDEN GODDESS taking my warm, vulnerable, exposed testes and applying cold steel to the sac and I fly awake scared, sweating, ejaculating, yet exhilarated because of my ability to dream these dreams.

One final fantasy, for I have kept you from your valuable and interesting tasks long enough, sees a man descending face down towards a woman lying on a soft bed, spread legged, welcoming him after hours of pain and torture. Oh, he moans, what pleasure awaits me and he continues to descend... legs wide apart, penis throbbing and erect and he begins to penetrate the woman's holiness but his moans of ecstasy turn to screams and an attempt to pull back... he cannot for he descends into the HOLY OF HOLIES but there is inside a leather cup with pins all round and four sharp knives like objects at 2-4-8-10 o'clock and when he has at last disappeared into her, she, with a demonic laugh, wetted lips, blazing eyes, in anticipation of what is to come – crosses her legs around his body and begins a sawing motion. The ecstasy of a minute before has become the castration of the present. He is no longer complete... he has been put asunder.

I shall close now... naked before your beauty, quivering before your majesty cruelty, frightened by your sadistic imagination and kneeling in awe before your glorious GODDESS-like nature.

LOVE, HONOUR, WORSHIP, ADORATION, LOYALTY, REVERENCE, DIVINE BEAUTY, THAT IS MY MOTTO FOR THE ANOINTED ONES, BLESSED BE THEY FOR THEY SHALL INHERIT THE WORLD AND KINGDOM OF MEN.

Please pardon all the typing errors and for them I shall go into my chamber of pain and redeem myself for all of these misuses of the typewriter and my male incapacity to achieve perfection.

Into my Victorian home of my dreams, with its torture chambers in the bowels of the earth where no restraint keeps you from doing your evil best and with the assistants needed to make it function properly, I leave you and remain until then your devoted slave,

Love,

O.K.

THE LUSTS OF THE LIBERTINES
The Marquis De Sade

The Circle of Manias, the Circle of Excrement, the Circle of Blood; three gateways to a living Hell envisaged by the Marquis de Sade as he simmered in the bowels of the Bastille. An infernal zone where Libertines are free to pursue and execute their every caprice, no matter how depraved or inhuman.

Here, in a brand new, unexpurgated and explicit translation, are the 447 "complex, criminal and murderous lusts" of the Libertines as documented by de Sade in his accursed atrocity bible *The 120 Days Of Sodom;* a catalogue of debaucheries, cruelties and pathological perversions still unequalled in the annals of transgressive literature.

DUNGEON EVIDENCE: *Correct Sadist II*
Terence Sellers

The Mistress Angel Stern presides without mercy over a New York dungeon where her slaves, the "morally insane" of modern society, obey her every whim and undergo any degradation she wills upon them.

In the closed confines of a torture zone, these paraphiliacs and sexual malcontents use her image as an object for their masturbatory depravities, craving her cruelty in an abyss of sadomasochism and bondage.

Here are the bizarre case histories, philosophies and psychopathologies of a dominatrix; a frank testament which reveals not only the drives which lead some to become slaves, but also the complex exchange of psychic energies involved in scenes of dominance and submission.

THE VELVET UNDERGROUND
Michael Leigh

Swingers and swappers, strippers and streetwalkers, sadists, masochists, and sexual mavericks of every persuasion; all are documented in this legendary exposé of the diseased underbelly of '60s American society.

The Velvet Underground is the ground-breaking sexological study that lent its name to the seminal New York rock'n'roll group, whose songs were to mirror its themes of depravity and social malaise.

Welcome to the sexual twilight zone, where the death orgies of Altamont and Helter Skelter are just a bull-whip's kiss away.

SISTER MIDNIGHT *Jeremy Reed*

The Marquis de Sade is dead – but his sister is alive and
well, stalking the ruins of the château of La Coste where
she reconstructs the apocalyptic orgies, tortures and
blasphemies of her brother's reviled last will and testament,
The 120 Days Of Sodom.

Castle freaks, killing gardens, lesbian love trysts on
human furniture; these and countless other configurations
of debauched carnality conspire and collude in a sundered,
dream-like zone where the clock strikes eternal midnight.

Sister Midnight is the sequel to Jeremy Reed's erotic
classic *The Pleasure Château,* a continued exploration of
decadent extremes and sexual delirium in the tradition of
de Sade, Sacher-Masoch and Apollinaire; a tribute to
undying lust and the endless scope of human perversion.

THE SNAKE *Melanie Desmoulins*

When Lucy, a sexually frustrated young widow, is
mysteriously sent a plane ticket to Portugal, she takes a
flight into erotic abandon which can only lead to death
and damnation.

Soon seduced by both a debauched Englishwoman and
her Portuguese husband, she sheds the skin of morality
like a snake and begins to act out her darkest,
uninhibited sexual desires. Increasingly depraved rituals
of narcotics abuse, Satanism and sadomasochism –
presided over by Bartolomeo, a Sade-like albino cult
leader – eventually lead to the total disintegration of
Lucy's ego.

At Bartolomeo's isolated villa, a shrine to pornographic
art and literature, she finally enters the snake pit...

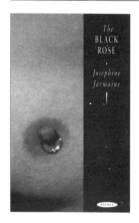

THE BLACK ROSE *Josephine Jarmaine*

Abducted to a mysterious French island, sixteen-year-old
Rosamund finds herself at the mercy of the Duke and his
four libidinous sons. She soon learns that her virginity
must be sacrificed in order to breed the Black Rose, a
rare flower whose aphrodisiac elixir will transform the
world into a polysexual playground of orgiastic and
orgasmic excess.

Rosamund's carnal initiation plunges her into a vortex
of pain and pleasure, as she discovers that the Château
Rose is a sensory realm where sadism, sapphism, sodomy,
incest, bestiality, bondage and rampant fornication are a
way of life.

The Black Rose is a stunning hybrid of decadence and
explicit sexuality, a unique modern classic.

velvet

PHILOSOPHY IN THE BOUDOIR *The Marquis de Sade*

In the boudoir of a sequestered country house, a young virgin is ruthlessly schooled in evil. Indoctrinated by her amoral tutors in the ways of sexual perversion, fornication, murder, incest, atheism and complete self-gratification, she takes part with growing abandon in a series of violent erotic orgies which culminates with the flagellation and torture of her own mother – her final act of liberation.

Philosophy In The Boudoir is the most concise, representative text out of all the Marquis de Sade's works, containing his notorious doctrine of libertinage expounded in full, coupled with liberal doses of savage, unbridled eroticism, cruelty and violent sexuality. The renegade philosophies put forward here would later rank amongst the main cornerstones of André Breton's Surrealist manifesto.

THE SHE-DEVILS *Pierre Louÿs*

A mother and her three daughters...sharing their inexhaustible sexual favours between the same young man, each other, and anyone else who enters their web of depravity. From a chance encounter on the stairway with a voluptuous young girl, the narrator is drawn to become the plaything of four rapacious females, experiencing them all in various combinations of increasingly wild debauchery, until they one day vanish as mysteriously as they had appeared.

Described by Susan Sontag as one of the few works of the erotic imagination to deserve true literary status, *The She Devils (Trois Filles De Leur Mère)* remains Pierre Louÿs' most intense, claustrophobic work; a study of sexual obsession and mono-mania unsurpassed in its depictions of carnal excess, unbridled lust and limitless perversity.

THE PLEASURE CHATEAU *Jeremy Reed*

The story of Leanda, mistress of an opulent château, who tirelessly indulges her compulsion for sexual extremes, entertaining deviants, transsexuals and freaks in pursuit of the ultimate erotic experience. She is finally transported to a zone where sex transcends death, and existence becomes a never-ending orgy of the senses. The book also includes *Tales Of The Midget*, astonishing erotic adventures as related by a dwarf raconteur versed in decades of debauch.

Jeremy Reed, hailed as one of the greatest poets of his generation, has turned his exquisite imagination to producing this masterpiece of gothic erotica in the tradition of de Sade, Apollinaire and Sacher-Masoch, his tribute to the undying flame of human sexuality.

FLESH UNLIMITED *Guillaume Apollinaire*

The debauched aristocrat Mony Vibescu and a circle of fellow sybarites blaze a trail of uncontrollable lust, cruelty and depravity across the streets of Europe. A young man reminisces his sexual awakening at the hands of his aunt, his sister and their friends as he is irremediably corrupted in a season of carnal excess.

Flesh Unlimited is a compendium edition of *Les Onze Mille Verges* and *Les Mémoires d'Un Jeune Don Juan*, Apollinaire's two wild masterpieces of the explicit erotic imagination, works which compare with the best of the Marquis de Sade.

Presented in brand new translations by Alexis Lykiard (translator of Lautréamont's *Maldoror*), these are the original, complete and unexpurgated versions, with full introduction and notes.

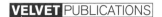

VELVET PUBLICATIONS

THE WHIP ANGELS *Anonymous*

Victoria's journal reveals her darkest secrets, her induction into a bizarre yet addictive sexual underground at the hands of her immoral, incestuous guardians. Behind the façade of everyday life seethes black leather mayhem, voluptuous eruptions of demonic angels from timeless torture zones, a midnight twist heralded by the bullwhip's crack and the bittersweet swipe of the cat.

Blazing with erotic excess and incandescent cruelty, *The Whip Angels* is a feast of dominance and submission, of corrupted innocence and tainted love. In the tradition of *The Story Of O* and *The Image*, this modern classic was written by an anonymous French authoress (believed to the wife of Georges Bataille) fully versed in the ways of whipcord and the dark delirium of those in both physical and spiritual bondage.

HOUSE OF PAIN *Pan Pantziarka*

When a young streetwalker is picked up by an enigmatic older woman, she finds herself launched on an odyssey of pleasure and pain beyond measure. Lost in a night world, thrown to the lusts of her anonymous captors, she must submit to their increasingly bizarre rituals of pain and degradation in order to embrace salvation.

House Of Pain is scorched earth erotica, an unprecedented glimpse of living Hell, the torments and raptures of a young woman abandoned to the throes of rage, violence and cruelty which feed the sexual impulse. Churches, hospitals, courtrooms, all become mere facets of the same unyielding edifice, a bedlam of desire and flesh in flame beneath the cold black sun of her own unlimited yearnings.

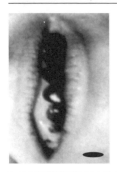

IRENE'S CUNT *Louis Aragon*

First published in France in 1928, *Le Con d'Irène ("Irene's Cunt")* is the last lost masterpiece of Surrealist Erotica. The author of this enigmatic and scandalous work is now known to be the great Surrealist Louis Aragon. Like Georges Bataille's *Story Of The Eye*, written the same year, *Irene's Cunt* is an intensely poetic account, the story of a man's torment when he becomes fixated upon the genitalia of an imaginary woman and is reduced to voyeuristically scoping 'her' erotic encounters.

In between describing various events in brothels and other sexual adventures, Aragon charts an inner monologue which is often reminiscent of Lautréamont, and of Artaud in its evocation of physical disgust as the dark correlative to spiritual illumination. This new edition features an exceptional and completely unexpurgated translation by Alexis Lykiard, and includes complete annotation and an illuminating introduction.

PSYCHOPATHIA SEXUALIS *Krafft-Ebing*

Lustmurder, necrophilia, pederasty, fetishism, bestiality, transvestism and transsexuality, rape and mutilation, sado-masochism, exhibitionism; all these and countless other psychosexual proclivities are detailed in the 238 case histories that make up Richard von Krafft-Ebing's legendary *Psychopathia Sexualis*. Long unavailable, this landmark text in the study of sexual mania and deviation is presented in a new, modern translation highlighting the cases chosen by Krafft-Ebing to appear in the 12th and final edition of the book, the culmination of his life's work compiled shortly before his death.

An essential reference book for those interested in the development of medical and psychiatric diagnosis of sexual derangement, the *Psychopathia Sexualis* will also prove a fascinating document to anyone drawn to the darker side of human sexuality and behaviour.